Army of Blood and Stone

John Urbancik

Army of Blood and Stone

John Urbancik

Army of Blood and Stone

John Urbancik

CHAPTER 1

It looked like any other empty lot, if a little oversized. Posters and plywood had been plastered over the chain link fencing to hide the eyesore of holes, pipes, and wires. It appeared as though the cathedral that used to be there had just been cut out of the city. This was the wound that remained.

This was where Pierce prepared his work. The boy in the gag and handcuffs watched intensely as Pierce sharpened his knives. He wasn't a precision cutter. He would describe himself as something of a hack.

"You're probably too young to remember the cathedral," he said to the boy, a scrawny college kid who had already given up struggling. "It was brilliant. I was here, inside the cathedral, sleeping in the choir, when a demon came crashing through the rose window. I've never seen anything so beautiful since. That explosion of red and blue glass—well, I'm afraid your blood will pale in comparison."

The boy struggled more then. He knew the knives were meant for him, but as Pierce lifted one of the longer, thinner blades and examined it in the sunlight, the reflected sun burned in his eyes, a strange prelude to what he knew was coming. He'd resigned himself to it, but he had to make a last stance in an effort to save himself.

It was pointless, but inevitable. The cuffs were unforgiving. The chain that bound him to one of the last bits of remaining stonework was strong and not very long. Pierce had driven the anchor into the stone himself before even selecting the boy.

The gargoyle had been made of this same stone.

It just needed a little bit of blood. Pierce looked at the boy, whose name he had never bothered to learn, and offered his kindest smile.

When he was done, when the ground had drunk up the boy's blood, when all that remained chained to the stone was the boy's wrists whilst the rest of him had been fed into the ceremony, Pierce sat in silent contemplation and waited out the day. The sun never fell quickly enough in the city. Long shadows stretched over the whole lot, falling through the crevices and holes and pits even when the sun was high, but when at last darkness arrived, the dark of a city that was never truly dark, Pierce took a deep breath and rose to his feet.

The blood had dried on his hands and on his implements. He wiped some of that off his fingers. It fell away in flakes but also lingered. The offering had been made. The promise fulfilled. The sacrifice completed.

He walked to the edge of the hole he had dug. It was only about two feet in diameter and maybe three feet deep. Not enough for a proper burial. The ground here, once consecrated and maybe maintaining some aspect of that, had been tough to dig through. Granite. Concrete. Asphalt.

The hole was symbolic, anyway.

The cathedral, long gone, had once housed numerous statues. Saints adorned the inside and guarded the doors outside. Gargoyles of all types had funneled storm water from the walls. One gargoyle had been built on the inside. Pierce had done what research he could into the cathedral, but records were scant. The local diocese opened nothing to the public, and his friend, the priest, had been uninterested in infiltrating that far.

There were few records of St. Lazarus' Cathedral and fewer pictures, but Pierce had been inside to witness the movement of that gargoyle. Its flight. Its confrontation with the demon.

He'd learned much since then. He'd been young, some twenty years younger than now, an opportunistic thief, and he'd taken a small piece of that gargoyle with him.

He didn't know if any of its life had continued inside that stone. It seemed the physical presence of the man had been birthed from the gargoyle remnants just in time to die.

He wore that sliver of stone on a chain around his throat.

He touched it now as he looked into the hole.

Pierce didn't have skills as a sculptor. He'd bought the little gargoyle at a yard somewhere upstate. There'd been plenty of fountains, sundials, and other lawn ornaments, and this was maybe the smallest of them, but it was intended as a proof of concept.

The gargoyle stood all of twelve inches tall. Heavy lids shielded its eyes because it was always watching, though there was nothing to watch inside the hole but darkness. Pierce shined his flashlight onto the thing's head.

It remained still.

Pierce knelt beside the hole and spoke gently. "It's okay," he said to the statue. "I fashioned the ceremony and the sacrifice to awaken you. I suspect you're tired and maybe hungry, but you have nothing to fear from me. I am—in a way, you can consider me your father."

To Pierce's eyes, the statue seemed to struggle to

maintain its stillness. It wanted to move. Wanted to fly, though those little wings would likely fail to lift it. It wanted to stretch its limbs and sink its stone teeth into human flesh.

But the gargoyle restrained itself.

By midnight, Pierce's legs were numb from kneeling and his focus was light. The sound of church bells, either distant bells tolling the end of the day or the ghosts of the Lazarus bells, roused him from the edge of sleep. He blinked, stared down at the statue, then pushed himself to his feet.

He followed a path that led underground, which eventually brought him to a subway line not far from a platform.

⚬━━━⚬

Eyes followed the man's path until he'd disappeared underground. Even then, the eyes remained still, content to watch and to breathe. It had been a long time since it had tasted a breath, if ever. The city air was stale and vibrant, filled with oxides and electricity and the pulsing beat of more than a million hearts just on this island.

When the man had not reemerged after ten, twenty minutes, then an hour and then another, the statue flexed its stony muscles, pried itself loose of the building to which it had been affixed many, many years earlier, and descended to the little pit where the man had left the statue of the gargoyle. The statue reached in, plucked the gargoyle from the hole, and held it close to its breast like a baby.

CHAPTER 2

Chloe woke in the early hours of the morning. Witching hours. Well before the sun even thought about rising, she was staring out the window of her one bedroom under-the-stoop apartment wondering why there was nothing to see but garbage cans. Was she supposed to put all that out last night? She forgot. She often forgot. It was hard to keep track of the days. Was she supposed to work today? Call her dad?

Why was she so awake at such an unforgivable hour? Looking at the clock, she could barely discern the numbers. They weren't numbers she should see.

Sitting on the edge of the bed, she tried to control her breathing, but a panic threatened to ride over her. She gripped the sheets under her fists trying to remember the important things. There was no one to hurt her anymore. She was safe. The nightmare wasn't just over, but it had ended more than half her life ago. Demons didn't hide in every shadow.

But that was all she saw through that window with the trash. Shadows. Darkness. There was nothing else to focus on. She closed her eyes and recited her poems and listened to the soundlessness of her apartment. There was too much stimulation. Too many lights, on the clock and her phone and the nightlight in the bathroom and all that city light falling in through the window. There was too much sound, even if it all came from inside her head. *I want you to be that mother, Chloe. I love you.* But also the sounds of grinding stone.

She never got away from that sound.

It crept into all her nightmares and all her silences. She grabbed her phone and punched up a playlist, it didn't matter which one, and sent it streaming through the little JBL speaker next to her bed.

She didn't have a lot.

She tried to keep things simple.

Inside her head, she saw—she saw things that made no sense, but she saw her son, her beautiful little baby boy, whom she had almost named Rick but the baby didn't have to be like him, never had to be like Rick, so she'd named him Stephen instead.

She had felt Rick's power in that baby, though, and his strength, even before she'd confirmed her pregnancy. Her father had taken her in. Her father had promised safety and sanctuary. He might have done all sorts of things instead. He had never been a particularly good man. They used to talk, sometimes, instead of yelling and arguing and fighting, but those talks never turned out to be good for her.

But maybe for little Stephen.

Little? He wasn't little anymore, was he? He was a man, wasn't he? Full grown? Almost full grown? She glanced at her wrist, though she wore no watch, and it wouldn't have told her how old her son had gotten. When was the last time she'd seen Stephen? His birthday? Which one? Seventh? Thirteenth?

He had to be now about as old as Rick the day he'd died.

Chloe's stomach twisted in multiple knots. She clutched it, remembering the feel of Stephen growing inside her. They'd had to cut him out of her. She nearly died. She'd lost so much blood. She'd never been the same after. Weak, they said. Fragile. Eat more, they told her. Drink more water. Take these pills. Don't listen to the voices.

She'd tried to tell them, even then, there had never been voices. Memories. They never believed her.

Chloe rocked on her bed until the grinding stone dropped to a simmer in the back of her head, then went to her closet and pulled out whatever would work. Leather jacket. Black jeans. She didn't need to impress. She wasn't looking for something to take the edge off. She woke with a desperate need to see the place.

Her memories were real. That was the worst of it.

She wore heels anyway and took extra time to get her makeup right. She closed her eyes, trying to let herself go into the music, but that never worked and it wasn't likely to work tonight.

Tonight of all nights.

What was tonight? It wasn't Stephen's birthday, was it? Had she missed another? Had she missed her own? Was it some sort of anniversary? It couldn't be that. A death day? The day the stones fell? The day the doctors told her Rick's baby was going to kill her unless they did something about it now?

She strut out of her apartment like a woman possessed. Maybe there was some truth to that. She walked like she had intentions. A place to be. She hit the pavement and walked because nothing but the noise of the city would drown the white noise stone grinding in her head. She passed a park. She passed a deli. She passed a variety of clubs just getting started for the night.

Maybe later, she promised herself.

Maybe later.

She worked because it was good to have something to focus on, but that didn't always work out for her and she flitted from one job to another despite that her father paid all her bills. "I want you safe," he told her once. "I want you comfortable."

She shook her head. He'd never said anything about wanting her to be happy. She wasn't happy. She didn't even know if she could be happy. Was that a real thing? Had she felt it ever before? It was only ever fleeting. When she was with Rick. When she was on X. When she felt Stephen's kicks inside her.

When her father said he'd make sure his grandson was well cared for.

She kicked out at the city, striking nothing but air. She turned a corner, another corner, and though anyone watching her would've thought she'd been strung out on something and didn't know where she was going, she found the boards and chain link that prevented the world from having to see the place where that cathedral had stood.

She would've gone to Brooklyn, but she'd have to take the subway and she didn't want to do that in the middle of the night. It was too long a ride. Too far a distance. She didn't know which train to take. She could never keep the letters straight. She might end up in Woodside again, in Queens, and what would she do then? She didn't even know a good place to get a drink in Queens.

Her father had bought Rick's old warehouse there. It had taken some maneuvering on his part, but after the police were done with it no one could come up with a reason why she shouldn't have it.

But it didn't matter where she went. The cathedral, the missing cathedral, was as good a place as any. Here, at least, the sounds in her head dimmed some, though they never went fully away. They would never leave her.

She found a place where she could peek through a hole in the plywood. There were multiple layers of fencing around the former cathedral. That had been a mystery, to her and to everyone else, the day it simply disappeared.

But before that, there'd been a gargoyle. That thing might have saved her life. Might have saved her then unborn son's life. Might have saved a lot of lives, but it ruined hers. Ever since, she imagined the visage of the gargoyle coming at her in all the darkest shadows. She heard the stone grinding against stone as it moved. She felt its cold, hard, deadly talons piercing her chest.

That had never happened.

But it might have. All sorts of things might have happened. She'd given herself to a faux vampire that night. She'd begged him to change her. She'd been so naïve. So stupid. She'd been changed, immortality didn't last forever, and the city shadows continued to hide the darkest secrets.

Even now, as she stared through that little hole in the wood at an empty lot that should have been just ruined pipes and part of a foundation, she saw something she never expected. Something she hardly believed was real. A statue, another statue, like the gargoyle but very unlike it, didn't stand in the distance. It moved. It cradled a baby gargoyle. It cooed at it, in a raspy, gravel voice.

The statue appeared to be a woman in a flowing stone gown with angelic wings.

Chloe blinked. She distrusted her senses at even the best of times.

"It'll be alright, little one," the statue was saying. The voice, though distant, was unmistakable. It wasn't a real thing and it wasn't a real voice. It couldn't really be drawing breath, could it?

And that thing in her arms?

Chloe shuddered. She pulled herself sharply away from the hole and put her back to the plywood. She stared at the buildings across the street and the lights of the cars passing. She listened for a sound, any sound, even the grinding of stone, but it seemed even her own psychoses had abandoned her.

Somehow, she didn't start hyperventilating. She gathered enough control of herself to turn back to the hole and looked in again.

Nothing.

There was no statue.

Her mind had played a trick on her. A cruel trick. Probably stole something from her memory. It must've been an anniversary to do with her Stephen. Maybe a birthday. He must be...how old now? Nineteen? Twenty? Maybe more, maybe less, but she wondered if he'd started to change yet.

Not in the way all boys changed to men.

But in the way his father, slain before Stephen's birth, had transformed from human to monster.

No, not a monster. Not some vague, unnamed thing that hid in closets and moved through shadows and killed randomly. No, Rick had been a very particular kind of monster, one that had deserved the attention of the gargoyle of St. Lazarus.

A demon.

Chloe was shivering again, but not because of the cold. She left the cathedral. She left that hole and the statues inside. Again, with deliberation, she wound through the streets until she found a particular late night place where she could drink and dance until dawn and maybe find someone to distract her from her own mind for a few hours.

CHAPTER 3

Stephen woke early. He often woke early. Mornings were the best time to get a jump on the day. Not that his days needed any jumping. He was in college, unsure as yet what he wanted to do, just getting his Gen Ed out of the way until he figured it out. His grandfather's grand plans for him still had time to be made real.

He just didn't know if that was what he wanted.

Still, he woke early, a habit instilled in him by his grandfather. He went for a jog, downed a protein shake for breakfast, and showered before dawn's light broke through the windows.

Classes didn't start till 8, so he had time to get in some extra reading. He was working through three books at the moment, one on mythology, one on history, and another on macro-economics. The myths covered all sorts of monsters and beasts from a variety of pantheons and religions. Often, as in Mary Shelley's Frankenstein and the original Phantom of the Opera, the true monsters of the story were never the monsters.

He liked to think that meant something.

Because he wasn't stupid, he wasn't naïve, and he knew his family history. He knew all about his father and his father's father. He had seen pictures. His grandfather started telling Stephen the stories before he could read and gave him everything he possibly could. Newspaper clippings were now all stored digitally. He reviewed eye witness accounts multiple times a year. He saw the signs in himself.

He knew of the church, too, a cathedral wiped off the earth by the quiet wrath of God.

No one ever offered a better explanation. The land remained unused to this day.

He used to stare into the mirror and repeat, like some sort of incantation, "I am not my father. I am not my father." Over and over again until his throat was raw.

When he asked his mother, she never wanted to talk about it.

His grandfather hadn't been an eyewitness. He hadn't seen anything. There were maybe three such witnesses in the world. Stephen's mother was one, but she was anything but sane.

There was also the priest, the one reporters spoke to, who denied any knowledge of what had happened that night. A rose window shattered. Blood and stone all over the transept and nave, pews splintered, and one Father O'Leary who'd claimed to sleep through all of it.

He was especially interesting because he'd still been at St. Lazarus' Cathedral the day God took it. He'd been questioned again then, but his stories were all the same.

His stories were all bullshit.

As far as Stephen could tell, the priest had vanished shortly after the cathedral. Maybe the church reassigned him someplace far away, like Bolivia or Tanzania, where no American reporters would bother trying to get their hands on him. Not even his grandfather's money had ever turned up anything solid about him in the past ten years or more. Just whispers of Midnight.

That left the artist.

He knew about the artist because of his mother. "Your daddy thought she might be some kind of angel. But she was there that night. To oversee his murder."

His mother was always dramatic like that. Telling stories of his father's murder to a seven year old.

Stephen knew better.

His mother was, for lack of a sufficiently precise medical term, cracked. Her versions of what had happened could not be fully trusted. Oh, there was truth underneath it all somewhere. Hideous and unspeakable truths. She tried to make words of them, but her mind wasn't equipped to handle anything so sophisticated.

There was nothing to confirm the artist had ever been there. His mother had described her as white-haired, but no articles about the cathedral — no articles about what they called vandalism, and no stories about its disappearance — made any mention of an artist. There were only his mother's tales. She didn't even have a name.

But Stephen did. He'd been researching this all his life. About ten years ago, after God swallowed the cathedral, a New York City artist became mildly and briefly popular with her paintings of cathedrals, unreal landscapes, and gargoyles.

An artist named Neve Spirito.

After her brief popularity, she'd disappeared from the public eye. Stephen had found articles about her in The New Yorker where she talked about the motives and influences behind paintings like the gargoyle. He'd always thought they'd had the air of truth about them, but there was a lot not being said.

Sitting in his apartment, bathing in the morning light and holding that mythology book folded shut in his hands, Stephen listened to the city, the rhythm of traffic, the horns, the winds. The music of New York came at him like a symphony, and he heard every note.

His senses had always been acute, but they were getting sharper and more intrusive. His dreams, the red dreams that had haunted him for as long as he could remember, grew more intense. He didn't have his father to guide him. He didn't know what all to expect.

He set down the book, tightened his fists, looked at those hands, the veins visible in his wrists, the muscles rippling in response to his slightest thought. If he closed them hard enough, he might crush his own bones. He didn't know what would happen if this continued uncontrolled. He didn't know how to protect himself.

With a sigh, Stephen picked up the book again and, without meaning to, crushed the hardcover's spine in his hand. He growled from someplace deep, a guttural sound he felt in his belly and in his bones. He'd never made such a sound before.

He got up from his couch. He dropped the pulped remains of the book and stepped back in horror. The muscles in his hands throbbed. Pain shot through his body, through every muscle and sinew he had. It rippled, then subsided, and if he'd ever questioned the validity of his grandfather's warnings and even his mother's stories, he knew it had all been true.

Monsters were real.

He was becoming one of them.

CHAPTER 4

In dreams, the statue had explored the city. She maintained memories of her life but didn't want them and didn't need them. Instead, she reveled in the marvels of the modern world, even if she couldn't understand them. Automobiles took a while to get used to. Computers? She knew they existed but didn't know why.

One thing she did know: she missed her sense of touch.

Since being trapped within the confines of this statue, whose body matched the one she'd had in life in tone if not in fact, she'd had only sight and sound to get her through the years.

The little gargoyle clung to her breast as though it might feed, but it needed no milk and she would never produce again. She felt it clutching her, but she felt little else. Was it cold? Hot?

She missed the touch of a man.

She brought the gargoyle with her as she soared over the city. Her wings were monstrous. She wondered what her face looked like. She passed close between apartment buildings. She crossed the river low over a wide bridge. Brooklyn. She knew it because of the years she'd spent exploring the city in her dreams.

She followed the elevated train as far as it would go, then continued south, reveling in the lights that sparkled ultraviolet through the pre-dawn night. She sensed the position of the sun, just below the horizon, in a way she didn't understand senses. They didn't work now like they had when she'd been alive.

When she'd been alive...

What did that make her now? She'd never felt more alive, and she would prove it. She reached Coney Island, the Cyclone and the Wonder Wheel, Luna Park, the boardwalk and the sand. She ignored most of the people on the streets, deliverymen and bakers and the like, but a lone man stood at the water looking out onto the Atlantic as if searching for mermaids.

She passed just a few meters above him. He must've felt her wind if he didn't see her. She dove into the Atlantic.

The water was dark. Murky. Hard to see through but not impossible to maneuver in. In this way, she confirmed that she didn't need to breathe. The little gargoyle seemed unbothered. She turned herself around, settled on the sandy floor, and strode toward shore.

She must've risen from the water like a nightmare.

The man stood there in dark pants and a white button shirt with the sleeves folded up and the top few buttons undone. He hadn't shaven in days. His black shoes had lost their shine.

He stared at her with an expression mixing relief and terror.

She flexed her wings, shaking off ocean water, and opened up her arms. She didn't feel the cold of the ocean or the pull of the riptide, but somewhere inside her, a stony heart beat one time, then a second, as she approached him.

An empty bourbon bottle lay in the sand at his feet.

She had never tasted bourbon. She wondered what it would be like. She bent to pick up the bottle, but she shattered the fragile glass without even trying.

The man stood his ground. "She sent you, didn't she?"

"She?" Hers was the voice of gravel and stone. It grated through her throat, but the sound was intelligible enough for the man to tilt his head and get this quizzical expression. She had stopped within arm's length of him. Up close, she saw the moisture under his eyes.

She had to look down at him. She was easily a full head taller. She hadn't been this close to a man, to anyone, in so very long.

He reached toward her, as though wanting to touch her, but trembled. He was afraid. Of course he was afraid. He should be. She grinned wickedly, then reached out and snatched him by the waist.

He might have been a strong man.

But her hands were stone and unyielding and extraordinarily powerful. She dragged him to her, cracking his ribs as she did so, then lifted him off his feet to kiss him.

She barely felt his mouth.

It was not a satisfying kiss. Not at all.

She flung him away from her. Blood poured from his nose and his lips. He tumbled through the sand making little noises of pain. She liked the sound of that. She liked the sound of his bones breaking. He bled under his shirt, too, and from several fingers on both hands.

Her kiss had cracked his jaw and broken teeth. It hung loosely from his mouth now. She hadn't even noticed.

"She," the statue said, "did not send me. I did."

She advanced on him again. He wasn't smart enough to run, or the pain of broken bones prevented it. Either way, she knelt, knees on either side of his hips, straddling him. She felt, in a faraway kind of way, as he protested. He wriggled beneath her. Pushed with his hands. Tried to dislodge her with a thrust of his hips.

Tightening her knees, she crushed pelvic bones and the base of his spine. He cried out this time, no longer a weak, meager noise but an honest scream, and her heart pounded two, three, four more times before falling still.

Her stone heart within her stone body.

She didn't need it.

She bent low over him. She would've pressed her stone breasts into his chest, but she'd forgotten about the little gargoyle there. Its back broke through his skin and bones and killed him much too quickly.

<hr>

Pierce went over the ceremony in his head. He had built it around a sound foundation, taking from the Aztecs, the Byzantines, the Celts, and Native American folklore. As sunrise drenched the city in the color of blood, an epiphany struck him. The kind of magic he was trying to perform was primarily about intention, but it was also inherently sympathetic.

He had excluded Christian ritual from his machinations.

He'd gone to a site haunted by the ghost of a Catholic cathedral and thought that should be enough. Obviously, it wasn't.

Tonight, then, he would attempt it again. He had to return to the lot and prepare the space. Clean the remains of last night. Find another boy for the sacrifice.

But he knew he had done something right.

Before dawn, he returned to the empty lot. He snuck in through the underground just as he'd done before and returned to the hole.

The boy's blood had congealed. His waxen face was stuck forever in his death mask, a hideous and pale mockery of how he'd looked in life. Lifeless eyes stared at Pierce's feet, at the hole there, all of two feet in diameter.

The empty hole.

Pierce knelt. He reached in, but it was symbolic rather than meaningful. He had left a little statue in there. A gargoyle. His test subject.

He should have waited. Because obviously, he now knew, he had succeeded.

When he heard the scrape of stone on stone, he looked left, right, and all around him. That little gargoyle must be hiding.

"It's alright," he said. "You can come out now."

When nothing happened, he added, "You're safe with me. I'm...your father."

He didn't move. He didn't dare. He didn't want to scare the thing. He wanted to demonstrate that he was not a threat. That the statue could and should trust him.

If he had cast the spell properly, he should have dominion over the thing. His commands should compel it. He'd wanted to give it a chance to come out of the darkness of its own accord, but he'd used up all his patience already.

He said, "Show yourself."

The shadows around him shimmered with movement.

It was too dark. Pierce felt suddenly uneasy. The statue hadn't been so big as that. Who else had come into his space?

A stone dog emerged from the shadows.

A golden woman like an angel.

A young girl with a bowl.

A lion-like thing with wings.

Hideous little gargoyles, twisted dwarves and long-necked snakes, squatted in the shadows, dis-formed eagles, and one so old its features looked like they'd melted in a Dali painting.

CHAPTER 5

She felt the pull of the words. The command. She didn't hear it. It was too far away for that. But she felt it, and so did the gargoyle clutched to her body like a baby. She rose from the pulpy remains of the man on the beach.

The gargoyle mewled and leaned away from her, reaching northward with its stubby little arms.

She shook her stone head. Dust fell away from her. She said to the gargoyle, "No, dear, that's not for us."

She saw the line between them and the speaker. The commander. The spell caster who demanded their obedience. Tendrils of effervescence connected them to each other and to the man in that empty lot.

She touched it. Stroked it. Plucked it like a violin string. Its high-pitched sound reverberated through the night. The gargoyle made a sound, as well, something guttural and instinctive, so she snapped the thread connecting it to the man.

Her own remained intact. It was thin, practically invisible, nearly outside of this world. But it was a connection, and there were other connections, each sounding like a different note. Dozens came off of her, but the gargoyle's sole thread connected to her.

The gargoyle folded into her chest again.

She frowned. Once upon a time, she had lived a life. She wanted no memories of that life, no indication that it had ever happened, but maybe this was just such a thing. The gargoyle clung to her like a baby because it was her baby.

Her baby who had died with her.

Her baby who had been murdered with her.

She gathered her other threads and, in a single, decisive movement, severed them.

Each withered and drew away from her sounding like an orchestra crashing and the silence that followed. With each string, a memory dissipated, a face from her past, a name, a person.

Good, she thought.

She looked down at the corpse beneath her. She had made that, she and the gargoyle, but she felt no connection to him. She put a hand on the gargoyle's head and said, "Hush, now," though it made no sound, and knelt in the man's viscera to gently stroke the side of his face.

Briefly, they'd had a connection.

The absence of him, the absence of all connections, rang hollowly inside her, as though she was an empty shell. She knew better. She was solid, more solid than flesh and bone.

Dawn bathed her. As yet, no one on the boardwalk seemed to have taken any notice of the body she knelt in. Those morning people beginning their days didn't concern her, not individually, but she realized the folly of being witnessed.

She and the baby might have to live their lives in the shadows. That was fine with her. Her previous life had been in shadows, hadn't it?

She wasn't sure anymore.

She ascended from the beach. The baby cooed, a strange little sound echoing through its stony body. She raced across the city, paying little attention to the trains, the buses and taxis, the masses of people already moving. They made so much noise. Screaming, cursing, crying, whispering—it was ceaseless. Relentless. The noise didn't echo so much as intensify.

She crossed the water again, flying directly between one of the arches of the bridge. They were plenty wide enough for her, even with her wingspan.

Her wings represented feathers. Someone had spent a good deal of time and attention perfecting the details. She'd been immaculate from the start. Her wings stretched perhaps two yards in each direction but seemed thin. They felt light, though that was likely because she hardly felt the weight of herself or the baby at all.

She returned to her perch. From there, she could look down on the empty lot. She had seen the cathedral in all its glory. In a way, she missed it. What remained was ugly.

The morning light thickened, revealing vibrating blue and turquoise and indigo in places she'd never even looked before. Color shot through the whole of the city like veins.

"Be still," she whispered, in the way that she could, to the gargoyle baby. "Be still, and when the sun falls again, you and I shall make some new connections."

Chloe woke after sunrise in someone else's apartment. He was still in bed, his wrists cuffed to the corners, his chest covered in deep scratches burrowed by her fingernails. He hadn't bled enough, but she wasn't a murderer. She had been with one once and that had been plenty.

They'd been his cuffs. She found the key on his bedside table and undid one of the wrists. That was more than enough. He could handle the rest.

Before she got out, though, he opened his eyes. He looked at her in the way men so frequently looked at her. "Will I see you again?"

She shook her head. "The sex was good," she said quietly, "but not life-changing."

It hurt to look at the expression on his face, so she didn't. She left. She left without ever learning his name or telling him hers. He'd distracted her from her own mind, but only briefly. In the end, all the other things of the world came back to her. They always did. She'd slept briefly beside him, her head on his scrawny chest. Rick would've hated this man. Detested him. Not enough to do anything about it, though. Rick wouldn't have given him a second thought.

She wandered aimlessly. But as often happened when she meant to be aimless, she found herself at the empty lot of St. Lazarus' Cathedral.

She balled and opened her fists several times as she stared at it. She'd come from a different direction. She saw the emptiness where once there had been spires. The buildings behind the cathedral that she should not have been able to see. The chain link fence and wood panels meant to keep prying eyes out of this particular mystery.

The real mystery was why hadn't anyone done anything with a piece of prime real estate in the middle of lower Manhattan. The church probably still owned the land. Did they intend to bury the secrets of gargoyles and demons by not, in fact, burying anything?

She paced up and down a stretch of sidewalk across the street from the church. She refused to get too close. Didn't want to look inside again. But she couldn't tear herself away. She might have to find a shovel and bury the church herself.

Yes, that was the answer. A shovel wouldn't do the trick, but how hard would it be for her to use her father's money to get her hands on, say, a dump truck? That was the one with a scoop, right? If she leveled the earth inside, someone would see its potential. They could build a tower. A luxury apartment building. Why not another church?

How would that work? Would it also be named after St. Lazarus, or would they have to pick a new name? They could call it St. Rick's—no, St. Richard's. There were thousands of saints, surely one of them had been named Richard. He'd probably cured a medieval town of some plague, the Red Death perhaps, when he'd intoned the name of God and begged for mercy.

She didn't believe in mercy.

They might call the new cathedral St. Richard's, but it would actually be named for the demon that died there. That seemed appropriate. A sign of, not salvation, but eternal absolution.

She had sinned, too.

There should be a Saint Chloe. She could name the cathedral for herself, once she'd filled the holes and toppled the mountains.

A beam of light struck her from above. It wasn't the eye of God, just a bit of sunlight reflecting off a high window. She looked up at it, at the sheer gray of the city around her, and that's when she saw the statue.

The statue.

The damned statue she thought she'd seen last night on the grounds of the cathedral.

It stood at the corner of a rooftop and looked down on the city. Its wings reminded her of bats. Flying rodents rather than angels, because with a face like that she couldn't be an angel.

Chloe stared at the statue long enough to be certain it stared back.

That had to be wrong.

Chloe whimpered briefly. She knew what it was but she let it out anyway. That statue, that woman or goddess or whatever she was, wasn't alone. Another statue, a gargoyle, much smaller though Chloe couldn't judge actual size from this distance, clung to its chest.

It'll be alright, little one. That statue had spoken those words sometime late in the night.

The gargoyle shifted its weight against the other statue. It was a slight movement, possibly a trick of shadows from ten or fifteen stories below, but the sound of grinding stone was unmistakable.

It was a sound Chloe had tried desperately all her life to escape.

She had failed and failed, and failed again now.

She ran screaming.

The eyes of that statue stayed on her.

CHAPTER 6

The last of his classes ended by midday. Usually, Stephen would spend the afternoon in the library or computer lab. Sometimes, he visited museums and galleries, but today he had something of a mission.

He wasn't much of an artist himself, but he'd found a small gallery in Brooklyn that still had a Neve Spirito original on display. At least, it was there if the internet was to be trusted, which of course it wasn't. He worked the subways until one got him on the other side of the East River. He walked toward the bridge and Jane's Carousel for a bit, then veered to the right.

When he got to the place where the gallery should have been, he found an empty storefront window, railing down to lock it away from the city. The door was set in a little alcove less than a step raised above the sidewalk. It looked ajar, but he stared for a bit at the whole scene trying to make sure he was in the right place.

He cupped his hand above his eyes and pressed it to the window to get a look inside but saw only an empty room. There were a few panels that might have held art, but the place looked to have fallen into neglect.

Still, a few bare bulbs hung on cords from the ceiling. They were lit. And there seemed to be a closed door leading to another room in the back.

He checked his phone and the number stenciled on the door. He was at the right place.

He frowned. There might be someone inside. The lights were on and the door open. He knocked three times. The door moved gently, not far, revealing nothing but dark. No one answered.

He pushed the door.

It opened onto a hallway that ran alongside the empty storefront. While a doorway opened into the store, the hall continued deeper to another open door. A small pool of light spilled from there.

"Hello?" Stephen asked, stepping into the hall.

A stairway led upstairs, too. His eyes revealed nothing, despite his heightened senses, but he heard the scratching of what might be a pencil on paper. It came from upstairs. He called out again. Still, no one answered.

With only a breath of hesitation, Stephen started up the stairs.

They didn't lead to another hallway, but straight into a single room that stretched from the front windows to the back. A second set of stairs climbed further.

Near the back window, in a pool of sunlight that somehow managed to snake its way inside, a woman sat at one of several artists desks. All the flat surfaces were tilted at about 45 degrees, and each featured a backlight on a round disk that presumably could be turned in any direction.

The woman worked on such a disk.

A flat table beside her carried a number of pens and pencils, charcoals and conte crayons, and other assorted art tools. She paused, not putting down the pencil in her hand, and picked up the coffee mug.

At the top of the stairs, Stephen said, "Excuse me."

Startled, she spun on her stool. She was an older woman with stylized lines of silvery gray in her hair and hints of crow's feet at the corners of her eyes. She set the mug back on the table, swept a bit of hair from in front of her eyes, and looked him thoroughly up and down before saying, "You're early."

That might or might not be a complaint, but he was pretty sure she didn't mean him. "I'm here to see the exhibit."

"The exhibit?" She rolled her eyes, put the pencil down, and said, "I deleted all my social medias, and you people still keep coming."

"You people?"

"Whatever you call yourselves," she said. "Gawkers. Aficionados. Artists, even, sometimes. You don't look like an artist. Your fingernails are too perfect. And your eyes, too."

"Not an artist," Stephen said.

She shook her head. "I didn't think so. So you wanted to see something. The sculpture, it's all gone into Manhattan, shipped it off months ago. People stopped coming during Covid, and never really started up again. I didn't care anymore to run a gallery, so I closed it all down and got rid of most of it."

"I wasn't looking for sculpture," Stephen said.

She hopped off the stool, slapping both feet on the ground. "Yeah, no, I didn't think so. You look the type, but, I don't know, you've got something...in your eyes, I'd say. You're not here to pose for me and you're not here for the sculpture, which was what everyone wanted to see." She grinned. "Erotic poses. People ate that shit up."

"You the sculptor?" Stephen asked.

"Sometimes, yeah," she said, walking to one of the other artist stations. "Sometimes the model. You know how it is."

"Actually, I don't."

She shrugged as she opened what seemed to be a coffee table book on the side table next to that empty artist desk. "Well, don't be shy," she said. "You've already interrupted me and I ain't gonna bite." As an afterthought, she added, "Not without consent."

Stephen glanced at what she was working on. The image was turned not quite completely upside down. He almost didn't recognize it as two men kissing.

The book in front of her contained prints of photographs of the sculptures that had been there. Some were twice the size of the people next to them. All showed bodies twisted around each other in provocative—no, downright pornographic— arrangements that might or might not be physically possible.

In some of the photos, the people posing with the sculptures inserted themselves in whatever way they could manage. This artist appeared in some of those photos. She wasn't always completely dressed in them.

"Like what you see?" she asked.

"I didn't come for the sculpture," Stephen reminded her.

She stopped flipped the pages for him, gave an exaggerated sigh, and said, "Then what?"

"The internet says you have a Neve Spirito painting here. I've never seen one in real life, only pictures."

She met his eye and, with deliberate slowness, closed the book. She met his eyes again, this time taking her time, turning over whatever thoughts she had in her head. Finally, lowering her voice in both volume and pitch, she said, "I live upstairs."

She glanced up the stairs that climbed over the other and led to the third story.

"You can handle it," she said suddenly. She grabbed him by the hand and led Stephen to the stairs. She didn't let go as she went up. She moved faster than she spoke now, as if excited by the possibility.

Again, the whole floor was open. There was a stovetop, sink, and counter at the back windows, and a big screen on the side wall. Another set of stairs rose further to a small landing and a closed door.

But the focal point was definitely the bed. King-sized, it dominated the center of the space. It was perfectly made, silk or satin sheets that shimmered redly in the natural light from the windows. Iron posts rose from all four corners to a canopy. The curtains were open, and just as red as the pillows, but there were also rings for handcuffs or ropes or chains along both the upper and lower parts of the bed.

Near the kitchen area, there was a small dining room table. She motioned toward that table, and the wall behind it, where a painting hung. The portrait depicted an angel, head bowed and crowned by a halo, bleeding from its chest and still holding a bloody knife in one hand like the jack in a deck of playing cards.

"It's from her early period," the woman said. "Neve Spirito had several styles. Her landscapes are remarkable. The architecture she focused on later, especially her series on gargoyles and churches, was absolutely stunning. There's depth and emotion I only wish I could capture in my own work. Most of them aren't quite so...scandalous as this one. It's called *Angel 3*, part of a series, and I think she finished it just before she started the gargoyles."

Stephen approached the painting to get a better feel for the details. The three-dimensionality of the paint surprised him. It had been done in thick strokes of oil, and the details were applied later onto the ocean of paint. It looked different from every angle.

But it was before her gargoyles.

Even still, he felt blood pounding through his veins as he looked at the painting. His hands stretched at the skin around them. Arteries pulsed against his throat and in his thighs. His heart threatened to break through his ribs.

Stephen took a deep breath. He tried to hold back the transformation. He knew it was coming, but it couldn't be now.

He glanced at the woman.

She stood there with arms crossed over her chest and head tilted slightly to one side. She smirked, but he heard her heartbeat increasing and her breaths getting shorter. It was mild. She controlled her reaction better than Stephen did.

With another lungful of air, Stephen tried to push a sense of calm through his body. He'd studied yoga and tai chi and meditation in anticipation of this day.

She sucked in the corner of her lower lip. She glanced at the bed. She said, in a low voice, "Do you need something? Maybe a drink?"

Stephen tried to work his mouth, but it was too much effort to repress the metamorphosis his body so desperately needed. It had never been so nearly overwhelming as this. He fumbled into one of the chairs beside the table. He squeezed both his fists. His shirt started to tear at the seams.

She set a bottle of cold water in front of him. She'd removed the cap. That was probably good. He wasn't sure he could get his hands to work properly right now. He drank, lettering the icy water cool his throat and cool his blood. He inhaled deeply. Closed his eyes. And he exhaled in some relief as he felt the surge of transformative energy ebb.

He kept his eyes closed for longer than he probably should have.

He knew when he opened them, he'd find the artist staring directly into his soul, and she would see absolutely everything he'd kept so well hidden.

CHAPTER 7

Arella sat opposite the—what was he, a man, a customer, a patron of the arts?—she sat opposite him with a second bottle of water ready. He drank the first down like a man fresh from the desert.

She let him breathe. She didn't interrupt.

She'd seen the rippling through his skin, the stress on the fabric of his clothes, the momentary discoloration in his hands, the throbbing that seemed ready to rip through his skin. Clearly, he wasn't a werewolf, but she couldn't help thinking about any number of bad werewolf movies and those transformations.

She recognized the danger he represented, but she'd always wanted to have a story of her own. Maybe this was it? She didn't even know his name. Yet.

The thrill of danger went through her. Raised the little hairs on the back of her neck. She kept watching, but he'd done something to prevent the transformation.

It was not lost on her that it had been triggered by Neve's painting.

They'd shared much wine together in the past. Exchanged stories. Each to top the last. Arella hadn't always believed in Neve's ghost, gargoyle, and demon— it was way more complicated a story than Arella would tell—but she had to admit, something had happened to change Neve's art for the better.

She didn't know Neve then. It was, what, twenty years? They didn't meet until after they were both featured in that article in The New Yorker.

She wondered how Neve would react if she called after all these years.

The man who might be a monster on the inside opened his eyes and looked at her. He had the look of a caged animal. He wanted escape, which wouldn't be hard from here. She didn't want to lose him yet.

"I should go."

"No," Arella said, pushing the other bottle across the table to him. "You need to, I don't know, calm down for a bit first. Before you risk the streets."

"Risk..."

She shook her head but made sure not to look straight into his eyes. First, they were full of youth and vigor, and smoldering, and she was having a hard enough time trying to control her line of thought. Second, and more importantly, her eyes would be another bar on the cage. She didn't want to force a fight or flight reaction in him. If he fled, she'd never see him again and that would be horrible.

If he fought, she wouldn't enjoy it for long.

"I'm sorry I bothered you," he said, pushing the chair back.

She reached across, putting a hand on top of his wrist, a gentle touch meant to reassure but he looked down at her hand as though she'd tried to stab him. She snatched it away quickly. At least it stopped him from getting up.

"It's no bother," she said quietly but quickly. "I understand better than you think."

He chuckled.

Arella smiled. She put her hand on his again, not so sudden this time, and squeezed gently. "I might not be the beauty I was when I was your age," she said, "but I still know what soothes the beast."

He stared at their hands. His felt so hot under hers. It wasn't a sexual heat. When she took her hand away, she was sure it would be red. She might fry an egg on the back of his hand. That wasn't sexy at all.

"I don't know what you're going through," Arella said, "but I can see you need a friend." She paused long enough for a breath. "I'm Arella. I'm an artist, a damn good one if you believe the magazines, and I've...well, I've never dealt with anything like this before, but I know people who have."

"You didn't."

"You'd be surprised," she said. Then, not sure if she should and certain it was a stab in the dark, she added, "Neve told me everything."

He looked at her now like a child, like a puppy, like a man who wasn't sure if there was any such thing as hope anymore but had just seen an inkling of it. "Everything?"

"Everything."

"Then you know why I want to find her."

Arella shook her head. "She's gone, friend. Moved all the way down to Florida. And if you are what I think you are—she's not going to come up here for you."

"I need...her help, I think," Stephen said.

"I'll help you."

She gave him her biggest smile. She took his hand in both of hers now. She had him hooked. She was finally going to get her own story.

She would have to text Neve, anyhow. She wasn't a fool. There was plenty she didn't and couldn't know. Still, she repeated, "Neve told me everything."

"She...saw them, didn't she?" he asked her. "The demons? The gargoyle?"

"She never stopped putting them into her art," Arella said. "She painted them, she drew them, I think she dreamed about them every night of her life after."

She didn't give a lot of consideration to how much she was going to tell him. What use was there in secrets? "I know, because she spoke in her sleep."

⚬────⚬

They lined up for him. These were the statues he'd returned life to, about a dozen of them, all but the little gargoyle he'd been trying to revive.

Pierce paced a short stretch of real estate in the empty lot. He couldn't let any of the statues out of his sight. They were a motley crew. Some came more slowly than the others. None of them said anything, though that didn't mean they didn't make any noise.

He'd been more successful than he'd intended.

It thrilled him to no end.

The way he understood it, based on the interviews he'd read after and what he'd heard in the cathedral the day the demon and gargoyle had destroyed each other, the gargoyle had been human before being put into the stone.

Pierce had been unable to locate another statue in which a soul already resided, so he'd set about creating his own semblance of life in the little gargoyle's stone body.

Now, looking at them, he didn't know if they were conscious or simple automatons that wouldn't do anything more than obey his commands.

Late in the afternoon, Pierce decided to conduct a test.

He stopped in front of one of the statues. This was a small one, about three feet tall, with deformed facial features, but it had wings. He bent to look into its eyes. Did it see him? Did it even look at him? He couldn't read anything from the stony visages assembled before him.

"Do you have a name?" he asked.

The little creature made a sound, a grinding of stone against stone reminiscent of a cat's mewling. The thing tried to give voice to its name, if it had one, but words were beyond its capacity.

He'd already known that. He'd been asking them questions all day. He needed to test their obedience. "I want you to do something for me."

If the creature cared one way or the other, it gave no hint or indication.

Pierce took a breath, then said, "I want you to kill someone for me. A man, woman, child, I don't care. Go, find someone alone, someone close...and bring me back their heart."

The creature made a sound like a question.

"Just the heart," Pierce said. "I don't need the body. I don't need the head. I don't plan to do anything with it yet, but a heart, still beating maybe but definitely still warm...I can always use a heart."

When the creature didn't respond, Pierce said, "Go. And be quick about it."

The creature launched into the air. It spread its little stone wings, but there was no way those things provided any lift. The mechanics of the stone creature's flight were beyond him. But Pierce had given it breath—or the semblance of life, at least—by magic, so it was easy for him to assume that same magic made all things possible.

He looked at another, this one almost as tall as he was but without wings, and said, "Go another direction. I need eyes. Two of them. Be careful with them. Bring them back so I can use them, too."

Eyes, as the saying went, were windows to the soul, but Pierce suspected he could put them to other use.

The stone creature nodded once, accepting the command, then ran, disappearing into the empty lot. They were numerous ways in and out of the former church grounds other than going over the fence. This one didn't have wings, so it didn't attempt to fly. Later, he could test whether or not it could.

CHAPTER 8

As he waited for those two to return, he set the others to work. They obeyed, because these were simple commands. "Build me a secret altar," Pierce told them.

They set to work immediately. They communicated only with noises, grunts and growls and the like, but they erected something resembling a small amphitheater in a low part of the empty lot. They used the dirt, the rocks, and any bricks they were able to scavenge. They slipped into the tunnels below the lot and came back with iron railings, subway benches, and the kind of podium you might find at a library to support an oversized book.

He should've waited until later in the day. He'd given them no parameters, so they set about the work without regard to stealth. The sun had gotten low, which meant it barely penetrated this deeply into the city, but it was still daylight and this was an immensely crowded city.

"Stay in the shadows," he warned them. "Don't be seen."

It might already be too late, and they didn't acknowledge his commands in any way. Still, he marveled at the work they were doing, the speed and efficiency they showed. They created an amphitheater that could host a congregation of maybe a dozen in the two benches they'd retrieved. One was a dark wood with thick arm rests between each of four seats. They had pried it from the ground somewhere, breaking it apart at the legs. On site, they used small chunks of asphalt to compensate for the imbalance. The bench had been designed to discourage sleeping.

The arms of the other bench were lower, but it wasn't as long and would only seat three. The two together would hold most the smaller statues and gargoyles. None were as big as Pierce.

Then, the golden angel woman arrived with a spherical piece of glass. It wasn't an actual rose window, nowhere near the size you would need in a real cathedral, but it was colored and sported an art deco design within its ironwork. She set it at the back of the makeshift pews on an iron post.

It was dark by the time they finished.

And when they finished, it was a functioning altar. It might not be a Catholic altar. It resembled St. Lazarus' original in no way whatsoever. They had retrieved a book. Instead of a Bible, though, it was an ancient copy of The Book of Lost Fates.

Done with their work, they arranged themselves in the seats and awaited the service. There was room enough for the two missing statues to sit with them. The altar, a flat but cracked piece of marble on a pedestal behind the opulent bookstand, looked rough from any angle, but it was there for Pierce's use. They expected him to sermonize.

All of this pleased Pierce.

One of the statues returned.

He had expected the little flyer to come back first, but it was the tall one. It emerged from one of the underground entrances into St. Lazarus' lot holding each stone hand up and curled into something of a fist. The stone was wet with blood. When it reached Pierce, it held out both hands, turned them over so the palms would face up, and opened them.

There were two eyes.

They were not matched. They were different in size

and color. One had been blue, the other hazel. Pierce hadn't specified that he wanted them from the same source. He looked at them a moment, picking up one to examine it and found it rather distasteful to the touch. It was almost cool, but still retained a trace of warmth, and some threads of ocular nerves or veins or something at the back.

He wasn't an expert in anatomy.

The other was just the orb with an impressive array of red tendrils in the white.

Pierce returned it to the statue's hands, which had kept it well protected. "Hold on to these," he said, "until I need them."

The statue closed both fists around the eyes and took its seat in the stony congregation.

Pierce strode to the altar, climbing the step they had created to lift it above those pews, and stood behind the open book. He looked down at the words printed there, though they were difficult to read. He assumed the lettering was Syriac, possibly Arabic or Phoenician, but it was beyond his ability to decipher. The imagery, however, seemed appropriate. Etched into the page in what appeared to be gold was a temple altar featuring a haloed man with his arms upraised.

Pierce had seen preachers raise their arms in just such a way.

He did so now, then fixed his attention on one of creatures he'd brought to life, and said, "We are going to have so much fun, aren't we?"

They seemed to agree. If possible, they even seemed excited.

Then the little flying creature returned. It landed on the altar, forcing Pierce to turn around to face it. The thing cupped a human heart within its hands. The muscle still beat, faintly, but that wouldn't last long. The statue's facial features, carved to look distorted and absurd, were covered with blood.

In its hands, the heartbeat slowed. A second between beats became two, three, five, then ten. After that, it ceased. The arteries leaked the last of the blood it contained.

He stared down at the organ as his grin grew.

"Yes," he said to the statue, "this will do quite nicely."

He lifted the heart, turned to face his congregation, and showed it to them. "It's a long time since this spot of land has been considered sacred. But as of now, today and tonight and for the rest of eternity, with this sacrifice, I re-consecrate it in my own name."

He squeezed.

The heart was tougher than he'd expected. He thought he would squash it in a single attempt. Instead, he forced out several small splurts of blood, most if not all that was left inside.

He set the bloody mess on the altar before him and withdrew his knife. His hands smeared blood on his pants, but he always carried a four inch curved blade, like a talon, for this kind of occasion. The blade slid easily through the flesh. He didn't stab it. He didn't want to ruin the blade. He carved into the organ, cutting it roughly in half, then cut each of those into halves again, rendering the pieces too small and slippery to easily cut further.

He set the knife down on the altar, nodded quickly at the flying creature that had brought it, then faced his stony congregation. "Together," he said, "we will change the face of this city."

CHAPTER 9

Chloe escaped into sleep. There was nothing else to do. She'd sought out someone, anyone, who might drive the voice from her head, but realized quickly it was pointless. The voice would follow her like the sound of grinding stone that would stay with her forever.

So she retreated to her own apartment, buried herself under all the blankets in the corner of her bedroom, and swallowed a handful of pills meant to ease her mind and let her sleep. They never worked. They usually put her on edge instead. They forced her to focus on a single thing, usually the thing that scared her most, rather than let her mind run free. But she needed the softness they provided to the edges of her perception.

She swallowed them with a good amount of bourbon.

The memories returned like shadow puppets on the back of her eyelids, everything tinted red reflecting the blood of her own retinas. Gargoyles, demons, screaming babies. At one point, she tried to reach out and grab the infant, her own infant, but her father was there shaking his head. He took the child away on the back of a motorcycle, which never could have happened because her father had never been on a bike of any sort, but they raced away toward the corners of her vision so the demon could step forward and dominate her again.

She allowed it. Welcomed it. Reveled in it.

In her closed eye shadow play, the demon Rick shattered the gargoyle, then turned his attention on her. She focused on the claws. The teeth. The promise as he punished her for her doubts. He held her down, scraping her skin, denying her the release pleasure would bring.

Then, she was asleep.

She woke with a headache, her heart pounding, and her mind reeling. She tried to right herself under the weight of her own memories. Grinding stone. It'll be alright, little one.

She didn't believe it. Not at all. She found the half-finished bourbon and took a swig before calling her father. It rang. It did nothing but ring until the voicemail picked up. She didn't know what to say. She realized her son, hers and Rick's, wouldn't be there anymore anyway. He was older now. Not an infant clinging to the back of a Harley. No longer kicking and screaming inside her womb. She'd given birth to the demon's child.

When was the last time she'd seen his face?

She threw the phone across the room. It bounced off the wall. She wiped the tears from her face with the back of her hands. It sounded like stone.

She got up. In the bottom drawer of her dresser, inside a polished wood box, she kept an assortment of rings. She'd never worn any of them, not even the engagement ring—an emerald cut diamond in platinum. They had been the demon's trophies. Or Rick's reminders of the humanity he'd lost. She didn't know. She fingered them now, picking through them and rolling them across her palm, slipping them onto her fingers. Some were too small. Most were too big. One or two fit rather nicely if she found the right finger to put them on. They were bands of gold and silver, some with jewels, all with stories attached to them. Stories and names.

Rick had shown her these before the demon fully possessed him.

Then the gargoyle had come.

That changed everything.

Rick would be here now, still, if there hadn't been a gargoyle, a priest, a cathedral. If they'd somehow managed to avoid that confrontation, Rick would be here now to guide his son through his own transformation.

He might have made her like him.

She sighed.

She slipped the engagement ring on her finger. She liked the way it felt, though it was loose. It might fall off her finger on a dance floor or in some stranger's bedroom. Then where would she be? Estranged from the memories of her demon lover?

It helped her focus. She took another swallow of bourbon straight from the bottle. It did little to dull the aches.

She retrieved her phone. The screen was cracked to hell and back. She cut her finger on it scrolling through to find the number for Stephen. Her son who was not named Rick because, really, Rick had never been a good man. There was no Stephen in her contacts. She knew this, but she still had to see it and it still made her sad every time. That was her father's fault, wasn't it? Or was it hers?

Or it was Rick's.

She didn't know and didn't remember and, honestly, didn't care. She had found him once on one of the social media apps. She didn't remember them all by name but she still had one or two on her phone, didn't she? She did. She opened them. Ignored the messages. They were all men she had hooked up with or might or never would. They could wait. She didn't find him in the first, and didn't find him on the dating site, but finally she found him.

She didn't recognize the picture.

That didn't matter. She clicked the button to send a message. Private. Direct. Personal. She typed, "Call me, please. Mom."

At the end of it, her fingers were bloody and she wondered if she'd ever called herself mom before, if she'd ever seen him growing up, but of course she had. They had lived together with her father for years before she struck out again on her own. At her father's request.

She didn't remember if he'd insisted on keeping Stephen or if that had been her.

She hit send.

Arella stared at him and seemed to know what she was looking at. Stephen didn't even know. It unnerved him, but he remained perfectly still in the chair except when he drank down another bottle of water.

She had locked up the shop downstairs. "Don't go nowhere, please," she'd said. She came back with a cell phone in her hands. "Yeah, don't come today, I'm just not up to it." She paused a moment. "No, not up to that, either. Stomach stuff. I don't want you to see it, hear it, or god forbid smell it."

She'd gotten him another bottle of water as she sat, and managed to get off the phone quickly after that. She looked at him, shrugged, and said, "Models. They can be so...insecure."

He'd managed to press back the transformation again. How many times could he do that before he simply erupted? Who and what would he destroy when that happened?

Finally, Stephen asked, tentatively, "What is it you think I am?"

"In Neve's words? A demon, though I'm sure it's much more complicated than that."

"Why aren't you afraid?"

"Why should I be?" she asked. "I'm your friend, remember?"

His response to that must've showed on her face, because she quickly added, "Sure, I'm a new friend, the newest you've got, but...Neve told me things, all the things."

"Tell me," Stephen said.

She met his eyes, held them a moment longer than she should have, then said, "Your father, he was...I assume he was your father...he was like you."

"Or I'm like him."

She shook her head. "Neve described him to me. The human him. She didn't tell me what he looked like, but what he'd said, how he acted, what he did. He tortured her. You know that, don't you?"

Stephen knew nothing involving the artist.

"He tortured her. And when he killed that girl, the last one he killed, I think, he set her ghost on Neve."

Stephen had no idea how something like that would work. He reminded himself he was, at best, hearing the story secondhand. It might be more than he'd already known, but no matter how much Arella claimed to know everything, she hadn't been there and didn't have all the details.

"I know he was a..." Stephen hesitated to say the word, though his grandfather had always been forthright. "A murderer."

Arella leaned partway across the table between them and took both his hands in hers. "You," she said, "are not a murderer."

"Not yet."

"It's not who you are."

"What do you know of who I am?" Stephen asked.

"I'm an artist. I see things most people never realize they're showing. I'm...an observer, Stephen. I can see the strength inside you, the potential, the danger. It's exciting, a little bit, isn't it?"

"When I lose control," he told her, "I don't know what will happen. I...can't guarantee you'll be...I can't guarantee your safety."

Arella smiled. "The way Neve described him," she said. "Your father, I mean. She said he was the same person, human or monster."

"Monster." The word resonated so deeply, Stephen repeated it.

"Anyway," Arella said, "I have an idea."

"Why do I think I'm not going to like this idea?"

"Oh, you'll like it fine," Arella said. "Do you have a girlfriend? Boyfriend? Something?"

The change of subject was abrupt. "No."

"Good," she said. "Then no one will get upset when I tie you down."

He glanced over her shoulder at the bed. He had seen it when he came in, but looked more carefully now. In addition to the rings on the iron frame above the bed, there were more on the bed, alongside the mattress on the side and foot—which he could see— and presumably all around it. An iron chain circled the lower part of the frame, running through those rings, but there was some slack so that the chains could reach up onto the bed.

"You think that'll hold me?" she asked.

"The bed is carbon fiber," she told him. "The chains, too. If anything can hold you, that will."

He kept looking at the bed. He didn't want to see more details, but they were there. Multiple sets of cuffs hung on the wall next to the bed, some feathered, some leather, some pure metal. There were whips, restraints, harnesses, a variety of implements Stephen didn't recognize.

"You want to tie me down?" Stephen asked.

She grinned. She licked the edge of her top lip. "More than you can possibly imagine. But I'll behave myself, I promise." Then she asked, "Have you changed yet?"

Stephen shook his head. "I've resisted."

"We get you tied down," she said, "then you don't have to resist. We'll see how...strong you are, how large..." She paused at that, then shook her head quickly. "We'll see if the bed can hold you. If it can't, I'm not sure what could except maybe a vault."

The idea caused a ripple of the demon inside him to coarse outwards from his heart to his extremities. He balled his fists again.

"We'll see how much you're still you," she said.

A growl rose from Stephen's throat. It came with a hint of violence and sexuality. He liked the idea of the bed. He wanted to tie Arella down, instead, to let loose and ravage her. He wasn't sure how much of that was the demon inside him. He wasn't sure how much the demon inside him was him.

It would be a good experiment. He felt his control already slipping.

He got up awkwardly, pushing the chair back away from the table but also pushing the table forward. He didn't mean to. The veins in his fists and neck throbbed.

"Don't," Arella said, guiding him toward the bed. "Don't let go. Not yet."

Stephen could barely control his limbs. He followed where she led him, but would not have been able to move entirely of his own accord. She took him to the bed, pushed him gently toward it, and had him lay down.

She wrapped one wrist with a leather restraint that covered most of his forearm. She pulled it taut, to the side of the bed, then added a metal cuff.

She climbed over him to get to the other arm. The nearness of her, the touch, the scent, drove into him. The demon inside surged forward. He resisted. He squeezed every muscle. He tried not to challenge Arella as she restrained his other hand.

She bound his feet at the ankles just as quickly. She was an expert. She knew her equipment. She then pulled a chain across the middle of the bed, over his waist. He hadn't expected that. He thrashed, an unconscious and involuntary response. When he did, she somehow looped the chain under him, tossed it over his waist again, then secured it onto the frame.

She wasn't done.

Arella climbed on top of him, her knees on either side of his chest, and showed him the metal collar she was about to put around his neck. Underneath her, he felt like everything in him had gotten hard and sharp. Every muscle, every sinew, every bone. He took a breath, a deep one, and held it while she clasped the collar around his neck. She connected it to another chain at the head of the bed, essentially making it impossible for a man to lift his head more than a few inches.

For a normal man, at least.

Stephen's grandfather had told him many times he was far from a normal man. He had warned Stephen that the day would come when he might lose control, but that he had to fight against that. Resist. Put his faith in God. Whatever it took.

He pulled at every chain and restraint. There wasn't much he could do. Still on top of him for a moment, Arella looked down at his body with a mix of excitement and fear. The change was rippling through him, and this time there would be no holding it back.

"Let it out," she told him.

"Get off me," he said. Her proximity incited his senses.

She leaned closer and said, "Stop resisting."

"I'm..." He bit back the words because his mouth felt wrong. Bigger than it should be, and agonized by the shift. He felt the sharpness of his teeth on his gums. "I'm..." He tightened his fists, which had also grown. Every bone inside him burned as it cracked and reshaped itself.

For a moment, he lost track of Arella. He couldn't see or feel the bed, just his own body as it erupted in fits and spurts. The pain was incredible. It lent him strength. He heard something rip. It was clothing, first, but then the leather she'd used to hold him down. The metal bit into him, suddenly too tight around his ankles, his wrists, and his neck. He raged against it, screaming in fury.

Carbon fiber cuffs snapped bloodily away from his one of his wrists first.

When he pulled his arms to his chest, the bed bounced. He crushed Arella to him, but controlled himself enough to not break her bones or squash her like a grape. He could have. The power he felt in his own limbs was absurd.

The collar around his neck twisted and broke away.

He didn't think the ankle cuffs had held, either. He was free. He was free, untethered, and unleashed. The pain of transformation subsided, and he found himself staring up into Arella's eyes.

She held on to his chest with her knees. Sweat coated her face. Strands of hair clung to her. She looked at the broken collar. Stephen, the demon Stephen, pawed at it with one of his clawed hands. The claws were long, sharp, and unexpected.

Arella put her hand over his. His hand was at least half again its usual size. She twined her fingers between his, her palm on the top of his hand, and leaned closer to whisper. "You can control it, Stephen. You are in absolute control."

"I am."

"How does it feel?" she asked.

He didn't have to give it any thought. He didn't even need to give it voice. But he told her, "I feel good. I feel..."

He lifted his hands and, with a good deal of gentleness, at least for someone wielding the strength of a demon, pushed her down his chest, to his hips, so that she might feel just how powerfully the blood coursed through his veins now. He growled, "I want to fuck you."

She grinned down at him and said, "Yes."

CHAPTER 10

The sun dropped low, casting the western horizon in a fiery display that cut like knives between the buildings. The little gargoyle grew restless in her arms. The baby. Her infant. She shifted her wings to shield its eyes from the last vestiges of sunlight.

She realized, of course, she must be some kind of angel.

Had she always been an angel? No. She had spent so very long just staring out onto the world. She saw the cathedral, St. Lazarus' Cathedral, the day it disappeared, swallowed into a void, victim of circumstances.

She hadn't moved then.

She'd never moved before last night.

A new altar had been constructed within the grounds of the cathedral. It utilized bits and pieces of the city, of the physical church and structures beyond, and she could see the blood.

Blood had made the magic work.

Blood had given her—not breath, not quite—but life, some semblance of it, and another chance to do right by the little one.

She tilted her head to look into the gargoyle's eyes. The creature looked back at her. It reached for her with stubby arms and made a mewling sound.

"Shush, shush, my darling," she said, her gravel whisper carrying on the wind.

But the gargoyle didn't shush.

The baby was hungry.

She considered baring her stony breast, but there was no sustenance for the baby inside her. No, the gargoyle needed what she'd consumed on the beach.

Blood.

She thought the blood of the one who had awakened her might be particularly sweet. She had severed her connection to him so that he couldn't even know she was out there, but she worried that their connection might have been deeper than that. What if, when her creator's life ceased, hers also ended?

She looked at the statues in his congregation. The stone dog. The winged lion. The dwarves and the angel.

The golden woman, almost full size, has helped assemble his altar. She stared at him now with a countenance like stone, like marble or like glass, but it was something else. She wasn't the same.

This was another kind of angel.

But the angels owed their allegiance to her. All the angels. Especially golden women statues that should not be alive. Certainly, she should not be doing the bidding of one such as him.

He might be their creator, but he wasn't, not really. She'd been—if not aware, almost aware, of all that happened around her for vastly longer than this young fragile man had been alive. He'd merely changed her. Changed all of them. Those he gathered around him were older, too, than he ever would be, but weak.

Angels should never be weak.

"Yes, yes," she said to the gargoyle, stroking its head, free to move now that night had reached the city. "We will rescue her. We will rescue all of them. But first, we must do something about you."

The gargoyle stopped mewling. It grabbed her hand, wrapping its malformed fingers around one of hers.

"Food, first, of course," she said.

After the bookstore, Tyler stopped for hot chocolate. It was just down the road from The Strand and it always tasted good. He needed good. This whole journey downtown had been meant to clear his mind and lift his spirits.

It hurt, to see Ellie move on so quickly.

He had loved her. With all his heart. All his mind. All his everything. But she was never going to feel the same way. She'd made it clear. And she'd made it clearer after meeting Alexander. He was from Europe somewhere, Spain or Italy, some country where they spoke about love and romance with a depth of heart Tyler barely understood.

It didn't make him mad. He wanted Ellie to be happy. But Tyler wanted some happiness for himself, too, and he had truly believed he could find it with Ellie.

It wasn't meant to be.

He just wished it didn't have to hurt so much. In his over twenty years, he'd gotten used to the loneliness. The rejection, however, cut deep.

After the hot chocolate, after spending a hundred bucks on books, he wandered the streets.

He didn't have any idea of where he was going or why. Eventually, he'd have to get back to his room. Classes again tomorrow. Or the next day.

He passed stairs descending to a subway. He wasn't ready to go home yet. Or if he was, he would walk it, he would burn through the depths of his sorrow. The taste of hot chocolate lingered in the back of his throat, and that remained good. It didn't solve anything.

He heard a noise like a lost kitten as he passed an alley.

He didn't know where he'd gotten to, just that he'd shied away from people as best as one could on the streets of Manhattan. He paused, at the edge of the alley, alongside a line of parked cars, storefronts and lobbies with their lights down or their windows gated, and peered into the dark.

It was still early. He didn't have any fear. Anyway, it was a kitten, probably a kitten. Maybe a coyote. That would be something. That might be dangerous, but it wasn't impossible. Or maybe it was a baby some desperate mother had left behind because she couldn't afford to feed it.

That made him pause again.

He wasn't the hero type. What could he do with a child? Well, he could take it to a police station. He could open up his phone's GPS and find one pretty easily. There was probably one nearby, right around the corner, or even a hospital. No matter how bad her situation, a mother abandoning her child would still want to give it the best chance to survive.

But it wasn't going to be a child. It was a kitten. He heard it again.

"Are you okay?" he asked as he stepped tentatively into the shadows.

He saw nothing. The alley was wide enough maybe for a car, but not a big car, certainly not an SUV or anything like that. There wasn't much hiding back there. A copse of overfull garbage cans. Stray graffiti on the brick walls. A fire escape descending the side of one, black iron looking old and jagged. A streetlight, all the way at the far end. Roll-up garage doors. Puddles reflecting the dim lights from apartments on either side.

And a woman.

He hadn't expected a full grown woman. She stood in silhouette past the garbage cans. She looked down, at the garbage or something amongst it. Was this the mother? Had she waited until she could be sure someone would find her baby?

Tyler heard the sound again.

"Ma'am," he said, stepping forward, almost reaching for her. Close to the garbage cans now, he could smell them, the odor was overwhelming, all rotten and decayed, but he saw nothing, no baby and no kitten, moving.

Then he saw that the woman wasn't a woman. She was still as a statue. Maybe she was a statue? She wore wings of some sort. Fairy wings? You could get those in costumes shops he'd passed one since leaving the chocolatier, but these looked homemade, close to her back, almost invisible in the first moment he'd seen her.

She turned her head to look up at him. Did she smile? There was more light behind her. He couldn't see her features. She hardly looked real. He hesitated.

What he had thought was a rock, at the bottom of the garbage cans, moved suddenly. It unfolded its own wings, which were too small and couldn't possible give it any lift. It was twice the size of a pigeon, not any bigger than that, and stone.

Not stoned.

Tyler wasn't stoned, either.

The thing jumped up at him. Maybe it flew. Maybe it propelled itself with those wings. Its tiny hands came at Tyler's eyes. He jumped back and away, swatting at the creature, hitting it and confirming that it was, indeed, very solid.

The thing kept in the air, kept moving forward, smashed his head back against the brick wall of the alley.

He flailed at it. He tried to push it away like a mosquito. Like a fly. Like a fly bigger than any rat he'd seen but, coming out of the garbage like that, just as filthy.

It didn't get his eyes right away. It shattered Tyler's nose. The pain streaked through his body, but he didn't have time to react before one of its little clawed feet smashed his throat and, if only momentarily, collapsed his windpipe. He couldn't get the breath to scream.

Then the thing bit him.

It sunk its stone teeth into his ear, scraping Tyler's skull but coming away with only cartilage and flesh. It tried again, and this time yanked out a clump of his hair and scalp.

"Child, child," the stone woman said as she came closer. "Forget the head. Take the soft organs under its ribs. There's more meat there, baby, and less resistance."

But the child thing ignored its mother, drew back its tiny hands, and struck the side of Tyler's head. This time, it cracked his skull, it broke through to the soft stuff inside, and Tyler stopped registering pain at all.

It hit him again, breaking away fragments of Tyler's skull, yanking out bits of his brain and stuffing them into its mouth. Tyler's blood dripped down its face. It didn't even seem capable of swallowing anything. It was stone. It had no real throat. The brain matter spilled sloppily from its mouth. But the blood—the stone body seemed to absorb Tyler's blood.

That was the last thing he saw.

CHAPTER 11

After, exhausted and spent, Arella laid her head on Stephen's chest. She might never recover from this.

First, it was, beyond question, the absolute best sex she'd ever experienced, and she'd experimented a lot in her life. She'd found things that worked, but with Stephen—with the demon that he was—the degree of pure physical pleasure increased exponentially. She was at times breathless, at times helpless, and at times hopeless. He wanted what he wanted, which was raw and unmitigated.

But he was the promise of so much more. Danger revolved around him. It wasn't just in his blood, but in his aura, if she could believe in such a thing. Violence was coming, whether he sought it or not.

He slept now, inhaling softly, contentedly. There was a level of purity to his emotions, to his actions, to everything about him, that she'd never seen and never felt. In some ways, he was like a child, innocent, wide-eyed, seeing the world anew.

But she wasn't a fool.

Quietly, carefully, without disturbing him, she got out of bed and left him there. Naked, bloodied and bruised in all the best ways, she crossed her living room, found her phone, and texted Neve.

Then she wrapped herself in a silk robe, opened a bottle of wine, and poured a generous glass. It was early, but not as early as it had been. She glanced at the time on her phone and realized they'd—occupied themselves for more than four hours. It wasn't, realistically speaking, too early for wine.

She had no illusions of happiness or stability or any

sort of relationship with Stephen. He'd come here looking for answers, as there was no one, maybe no one, in all the world who could help him get through whatever was happening inside his body right now. For the moment, she'd helped him redirect that building rage into something productive, something absolutely wonderful, but that wouldn't keep him restrained. She was out of her depth and she knew it. She'd bought some time for him, and for her—if he'd transformed in front of her under other circumstances, he might have slaughtered her, not even out of malice.

He turned over, open eyes looking in her direction. He was human now, thoroughly, but she saw the demon under his skin, satiated maybe for the moment, but still roiling, undulating underneath, waiting for its moment to emerge.

"How do you feel?" she asked.

He didn't answer immediately. He was young. Probably uncertain of what she was actually asking. Under other circumstances, he might be right to second-guess himself. Finally, he said, "Calmed."

"Are you really?"

"I've been warned about this all my life," he said. "My grandfather, my mother's father, had thought he knew what to expect."

"He was wrong?"

"He hadn't seen anything. He only knew what my mother told him."

"Where is she now?"

He averted his eyes. A sore spot. He didn't want to answer. He threw his legs over the side of the bed as he sat up. He looked again at Arella and said, "She's here. Somewhere here. In New York."

"Does she know?"

"She's...got issues."

"Honey," Arella said, "that's the most sane response anyone could have in a situation like this, don't you think?"

He considered that for a breath, then nodded once. "I'd have to get her number from my grandfather. I'd have to explain things to him. I'm—not ready to do that."

Arella frowned at him. She considered options. There weren't any. She wasn't a detective, she was an artist. She couldn't help him find his mother or his answers. "I can talk to him if you want."

Stephen shook his head.

"I will help you," Arella told him.

He smiled. It was a genuine and absolutely human smile. No elongated incisors. No masked wicked intentions. He got up and started to dress. His clothes had been ruined, but not rendered utterly useless. It made him hotter. Sexy, and simultaneously vulnerable. It moved something in her. She inhaled between clenched teeth. Then she said, "I have an idea."

"This was my idea," he said. "To find the artist. Neve Spirito."

"Another idea," she said. "I don't know if it'll help any, but—have you been to the cathedral?"

"It's gone."

"It's gone, but have you been there?" Arella asked. She knew the answer. Even if the answer was yes, it was a no, not in any meaningful or significant way.

"There's no point," he said. "I've been there. It's gone. The priest is gone. Everyone connected to it is gone. I've looked, believe me I've looked, and the only thing I've been able to find is...the artist."

Arella got up. "You found me."

He smiled again. He had dimples. "I suppose I have."

It wouldn't help him understand anything. But it might bring context, and that had to be a good thing, right? She didn't even know anymore. She got dressed quickly, and smartly, not merely fashionably. There might be running or climbing or jumping involved. She'd seen the hole in the ground that used to be a cathedral. Everyone in the world knew about it. The big mystery. The cover-up. The theories and conspiracies surrounding it.

She had a feeling he knew all about those.

But on the spot where his father died, and his father's father, the line of demons behind him, his ancestors on consecrated ground—now that he'd transformed, now that he'd lost control, maybe there would be something more.

Neve had talked about her ghost. Painted the damn thing. Maybe the ghost of the demon's father might be able to tell him things he needed to know.

Maybe it would trigger Stephen's angers and fears and bring the beast out of him. If that happened, she wasn't sure she'd be able to tame the beast, not again, if his ferocious and unfettered sex could be considered tame in any way. But she was in this now, in her own story, her own adventure, and she would see it through to the end.

<hr />

Daylight waned. Chloe didn't know what time it was and didn't care. She wandered, avoiding the cathedral as much as she could, returning to its site over and over again.

After sending that message, that ill-advised message, that her son would never get and never answer, that might even push him further from her, as though there was any more distance to be had, she took again to the streets and stayed on them.

She ended up at the fence. The posters. The holes in the posters. The damaged land inside, the scar on the face of the city. Her blood was in that scar. Her blood was in the warehouse.

Several times, she thought of going to Brooklyn, back to that warehouse, Rick's place, his trophy room, his pit of violence and degradation. Sometimes, she missed him. She'd known what he was, what he'd been becoming, but she still wanted him. Longed for his touch. He could be tender at times. She remembered softness. Quiet.

No, she manufactured the quiet. That came after.

So she reached the cathedral first from the north, taking a roundabout path like a whirlpool sucking her closer and closer to certain demise. Then she stopped in a park for a while, on a concrete bench, where she could see statues and people and wonder if a taxi might take her someplace else, someplace far away, so she could escape the sounds of stone grinding against stone, the sounds of her heart racing, the emptiness left inside her.

She came upon the cathedral again from the east, though she had clearly meant to go down to the subways. The tunnels underground were like a different world, where a different kind of people existed, living and breathing like regular human beings, when in fact they hid the memories of demons and gargoyles and priests and criminals. Maybe someone would kidnap her, steal her away from all the things she couldn't get away from herself. They might bring her to Seaside Heights, lock her in a basement from which she could still hear the ocean, the boardwalk, the screams of people on the Tilt a Whirl, the echoes of that roller coaster Hurricane Sandy had devoured like a hungry worm.

She circled back around, trying to run away, and passed through little shops, places selling pencils or luggage or vape pens. She wanted none of it, and ended up again at the cathedral, this time from the south, and she began to fear there was no escaping it. She thought of the gargoyle, shattered into pieces, destroyed by Rick's father, an image she didn't know if she's seen, dreamt, or imagined. She remembered blood on the stained glass of the rose window, blood in the pews, blood on her hands. She wanted to wash herself, but there were no bathrooms, just public restrooms, toilets open to anyone in the world and there was no way she could go into one of those knowing there were still priests and there were still gargoyles and there were still men who collected the rings of their victims.

She reached the cathedral again from the west, where she could see the shadows of spires, as though her destiny and its were intertwined, as though there was a certain inevitability to it all. In sight of the fence, she checked her phone, her social medias, for messages or any indication her son, Rick's son, the demon's son — hadn't forsaken her. But there was nothing. Nothing that mattered. Nothing that was real.

So she went to the gate. She looked to where the statue of the angel had been, high upon a nearby rooftop, where now there was only the scar her absence left on the skyline.

And from inside the fence, she heard the unmistakable sounds of preaching. Amid the scratches of stone. Not just memories. Not just in her head. She approached a tear in the posters through which she could spy, and yes, inside, a man with his back to her stood at an altar that was most definitely not there yesterday nor ever before that. With blood on his hands. Blood like hers. She checked her chest, just to be sure her heart hadn't been ripped out, and briefly touched her lips to taste for blood on her fingertips.

There was no blood.

Not outside the cathedral grounds.

It was all him now. The preacher inside. The wicked wizard casting his spell to an arrangement of little statues and medium sized statues, nothing so big as the gargoyle in her memory, the winged thing that had never been meant to exist.

She might have cried. She might have made a little gasping sound. It might've been her heartbeat that gave her away. But the man inside, the preacher, who surely must've been a figment of her imagination, though in hallucinations she only ever saw echoes of the past so this was new and unexpected and dramatically unsafe — he turned to look in her direction. As though the fence wasn't there. As though it was twenty years ago when the cathedral stood against the street and you could look all around without obstruction. He saw her, and he narrowed his eyes, and he cursed under his breath.

But she heard him.

And she heard the grinding of stone on stone.

And she saw movement in the shadows, in the shapes, in the congregation made up of tiny little gargoyles.

And Chloe ran.

ARMY OF BLOOD AND STONE

CHAPTER 12

Chloe knew the city.

She didn't know it in the way most people who lived here probably did. She couldn't give a person directions anywhere, couldn't find a particular coffee shop or bookstore, couldn't even always find her way back home.

She knew it instinctively. She knew the holes where she could hide. She knew the tunnels underground, not just the subways, not just for where they led but for how they worked. Like snakes. Like creatures.

She knew the alleys. She knew where to find businesspeople in their suits and ravers in their goth splendor. She knew where to find the college kids with their beer and drugs and low inhibitions.

And she knew how to remain invisible. She could slip into any crowd, no matter the size, and simply melt into the background. She had run from Rick in the past, she had run from Rick's demon father, she had run from his angel and his gargoyle. She had run from cops and gangbangers and pimps who believed she should work exclusively for them when she never wanted or needed that kind of work. She had run from deals gone wrong. She had run from deals gone right. She had spent twenty years running these streets around the black hole that had once been a cathedral.

So when she ran, she ran hard. Her head cleared enough for her to slip away from whoever and whatever pursued her. They couldn't have seen anything. They didn't know the color of her hair or her shirt or her shoes. They were stone, it wasn't possible for them to have caught her scent, but if they had she would and could do something about that. There were places selling cheap knockoff perfumes that would disguise her. No one could track a person by the sounds of their feet on these streets because there were so many damned feet everywhere. The resonance of footfalls drove her mad, and would confound the hunters.

No, they needed to keep her in line of sight, but they never had her in sight. They never saw anything more than her eyes—not even both her eyes, just the one, the right one, in all its emerald splendor.

One green eye was not enough to track any quarry.

Two out of every hundred people had green eyes. She knew the statistics. She knew the percentages. She knew some four million people could be in Manhattan at this instant. She couldn't be bothered to do the math in her head, but that was a lot of green eyes just on this towering glittering island.

She knew better than to run away. She'd been running away her whole life. No one cared. It never made any difference. She never escaped. And the hunters, the creatures, the stony congregation born from the emptiness of a cathedral that existed only in her memories, would never expect her to double back.

So though she appeared to run away, Chloe came back around to the cathedral, this time with every intention, not sure what she would do but knowing she needed to know everything and more than that. Her Rick, her demon, who still lurked in the corners of her vision when she forgot to forget him, had died at this site. His blood had been soaked into its bones. And though she didn't believe his blood would spare her, she also didn't believe he would allow for someone else, anyone else, to touch her.

She had been his.

She shuddered at the thought. Sometimes, the fear came back, the horror and the terror and the certainty that he had never truly loved her or anyone. It wasn't his love that would protect her now. It was his possession of her. He wouldn't give her to someone else.

She rose back to the surface of the city inside the cathedral's walled off grounds. It took a moment to get her bearings. She hadn't been inside in the dark. Streetlights were plentiful in New York, and though their light into the cathedral's land, there were none inside. No workman's lights, though there was scaffolding here and there, and earthmoving equipment, and piles of rubble that indicated work of some sort had been done inside here. Maybe the church hadn't abandoned it. Maybe the priest lived here still, the priest of then rather than the priest of now.

As she figured out where she was, she saw the priest of now standing with his back to his makeshift altar, his gaze fixed on the tiniest gap in the fence through which he'd seen her green eye. Maybe she shouldn't have gone straight into its heart. If he heard her, if he sensed her, if any of those stone worshippers realized she was there, she would be in their line of sight. They would see her, and mark her, and follow her beyond the ends of the earth, into and beyond hell if necessary. There would be no escape. And no salvation.

She retreated into shadows. She removed herself from his line of sight as best she could. She held her breath so as not to betray her hiding spot. She whispered soundlessly under her breath. She didn't at first know the words she mouthed or why. They belonged to a prayer, maybe not a real prayer, maybe nothing you would find in any Bible, but they were a prayer nonetheless.

Realizing this, she stopped. No god would rescue her.

She peeked around the edge of her hiding place. If this priest meant to see her, she meant to see him first, thoroughly and completely. And if he meant to destroy her, she would have to destroy him first. She would find a way.

⚓

Chloe watched as the preacher's congregation returned.

It hurt her head.

She had seen a living, breathing, killing gargoyle. She had seen her Rick, her demon, in all his grandiose failure. But she had never imagined seeing a veritable army of stone things answering to a skinny, pasty-faced excuse of a man without muscles and without charisma. Why they responded to him, she couldn't guess. It must be something other than his negative magnetism.

The statues scared her. The man did not.

They returned one at a time. She had no idea how many of them there might be. The first three came over the fence—one some sort of predatory bird with wicked talons, another that was clearly meant to be a dog birthed from someone's nightmares, the third completely unrecognizable like abstract art that served some purpose other than aesthetics.

Art should be interesting to look at.

Another returned from the north. This looked like the caricature of a dwarf, something shaped to resemble a circus performer but with all its features exaggerated. If it was intended to be male or female, she didn't know.

Another returned from somewhere behind her. She

retreated, back the way she'd come, disappearing from the surface of the disappeared cathedral just in time to evade capture by what appeared to be a golden angel.

Briefly, she fought the urge to beg for the angel's help. But she knew better. There were no angels in New York City, and certainly not in thrall to this preacher.

When she dared to look again, they had gathered around him in front of the altar, all their heads hanging low. The sounds of stone grinding against stone were constant, and now in a variety of pitches and volumes.

It was enough to drive a sane person mad.

Chloe almost laughed at the thought, but that would've given her away.

She did not know if the dozen or so statues were the sum total of his army, but at least two were missing. She'd seen the woman and her infant gargoyle. The woman had been more angelic even than the angel, though something was seriously wrong with the way she spoke, the way she moved, the way she existed at all in a world that should never have given life to stone.

So at least those two were still out there, possibly together, and possibly more.

The preacher was saying, "She can't have gotten too far. How could you have lost her? Did you see her eyes? Do you know how many drugs must've been coursing through her veins?"

Not all that many, Chloe thought. Not nearly enough.

She closed her eyes. Tapped her finger against her temple. Thought of the TMS therapy she'd had. Drills banging against the side of her head. They cleared her thoughts, for a little while, so when she remembered, and when she needed to, she tapped the side of her own skull. Her fingers didn't have magnets in them. They couldn't possibly have the same effect. But she assumed the memory of the effect would be enough, at least for the moment.

What if her son came here?

Why would he do that?

Because Rick's son would also be a demon, and would be becoming a demon soon. Maybe soon. Probably soon. Maybe he'd already transformed. Maybe he was refilling Rick's warehouse with the trophies of his various victims. Another shelf of rings.

Impulsively, she touched the engagement ring on her finger. She still wore it. A trophy from one of Rick's women. An emerald-cut diamond that burned her skin like a fire agate rather than a girl's best friend.

Who called it that anymore?

She rubbed her thumb on the gem. It glittered and gleamed, and it bit into her, reminding her of where she was and what she had to do.

Stephen.

Her little Stephen.

Her baby.

He might come here, to this cathedral, in search of some sign of his father, his father's father, the only men in all the world who could have taught him anything. She certainly didn't know enough to guide him. She wasn't fit to be a mother.

Oh, but quite suddenly she had a thought. A unique thought. It had never occurred to her before. She knew nothing about the demon that was Rick. Maybe they were long-lived. Maybe they were eternal. Maybe somewhere, right here in New York City, Rick's grandfather still lived.

Like the three generations after him, Rick's grandfather would also be a demon.

She held her breath. The very concept frightened her. She could find him, couldn't she? She could put someone on it. She could use the Internet on her phone. Track him down.

No, her screen was cracked and left her fingers bloody.

It was a sacrifice she had no choice but to make.

No one but Chloe could do this.

She left the cathedral, the statues, the preacher berating those living stones for failing to find her while she was right there, twenty feet away, close enough they might hear her heart pounding, her breath, her thoughts as they spilled from her.

She fled.

She escaped into the underground. It didn't take long. She sat at a bench next to a tiled wall. She opened her phone and stared at the spider-webbed screen trying to figure out how best to begin this search.

ARMY OF BLOOD AND STONE

CHAPTER 13

Pierce paced in front of his congregants. There were other words that better described them. They were, essentially, like golems, from Jewish folklore or tradition, which would obey his every command but were probably limited in use and lifespan.

So he wasn't concerned with allowing them to see him like this. There was a witness, a single green eye through a hole in the fencing that allowed her to peek through. He barely caught anything about her. The gargoyles, the statues—whatever they were—they should have been able to catch her. Bring her back. In pieces if necessary. She might make a wonderful addition to the next phase of his plan.

He intended to animate something bigger.

Much bigger.

For the moment, though, the statues—they had all come back by now, hadn't they?—the statues had failed to catch her.

She could be any of millions of people.

When he thought he heard something, he looked in that direction but saw nothing.

Finally, he stopped pacing. Behind the altar now, he faced his little army and put a hand down on the marble. The heart was still there, in all its pieces, no longer beating and no longer bleeding, crushed and misshapen but not utterly useless.

"I'll have to cast a spell," he said.

He had the means. The statues had brought him back the perfect grimoire. He consulted The Book of Lost Fates, flipping through the pages. He recognized some of the languages inside but not all of them.

Fortunately, the book relied heavily upon illustration. No: illuminations. They were painted inside the book with gold leaf and India ink. Power pulsed through some of those images.

Here: a sunbeam through a mirror piercing a man's chest. There: a face with flowers for eyebrows and the shapes of hearts etched into his fancified facial hair.

On a page near the middle, he found a map. It was the rough sketch of a map, not any place in particular but easily transferrable to wherever it needed to be. He touched the page, read some words, recited ancient rhymes he only dimly recalled. He laid his palm over the map, closed his eyes, murmured a few more lines, then snatched his hand away as the page burned it.

Underneath his hand, the map had shifted. It wasn't quite Manhattan, but it was a decent representation of this corner of the island. He grabbed a chunk of heart, still wet, and squeezed it in his palm. He held it above the book. Closed his eyes. Concentrated on the image of that green eye.

He squeezed the already dead heart with all his might, wringing from it the final two drops of blood. They spilled on the book. The page. The map.

Eventually, he exhausted the poetics and exhausted his hand. He pushed the piece of heart aside and looked down at the book.

The page had changed again.

Under the map, there was an eye, clearly drawn from one drop of blood. The other marked a space on the map. A space that was hard to read, at first, since it included nothing like street names or landmarks.

But it soon became clear, because the image wasn't merely a mark. Faintly, almost not at all, a cathedral appeared on that spot. It was a silhouette, clearly representational rather than actual, but it signified the cathedral that, once upon a time, stood on this very spot.

The cathedral in which Pierce had seen the gargoyle and demon fight to the death.

The cathedral which was later ripped from the earth by unknown magical means. The more time Pierce spent here, the clearer the echoes of that powerful magic became.

The statues crowded closer to see what he saw.

Eventually, he interpreted it. "She's here," he said, almost under his breath.

The statue nearest him, the one which had brought him the heart, whose hands were still stained with blood, looked up at him and tilted its head to one side. It made a sound. It hadn't heard him. It hadn't understood.

"She's here," Pierce said. "She didn't run at all. She's here, in the cathedral, with us."

<hr />

Stephen followed Arella back to Manhattan. He was hopeful, though he didn't know what about. She wasn't going to prevent him from becoming the demon his father had been. He'd transformed. It was—horrifying, but also invigorating. And the things they'd done—

He stole glances at her. While they walked the streets to the subway, then as it made its way over the bridge.

Mostly, he stared out the window at nothing, at the underground shadow, at the echoes of other platforms and other tracks. People coming and going. The tiled walls. Secret messages in the graffiti not meant for him.

He noticed details he might not have before. He saw more quickly, registered what he'd seen and interpreted it, since his transformation. He felt an urge to let go, to release himself to the thing inside him. The thing that had consumed his father and grandfather.

But he only knew what his mother's father had told him. A man who hadn't been there. A man angry at what had happened to his daughter. He blamed the demon for everything wrong with her. Every decision she'd made that he deemed bad or misguided. He would have killed the demon with his own bare hands if he'd had the chance.

He was an old man now, but not frail and not weak. He might still have that killer instinct in him.

But not like Stephen.

And not like his father.

Next to him, Arella looked into him. He didn't know what she saw. He had some ideas, but only some, and he wasn't willing to believe them all. She was his mother's age, but still beautiful. The demon in him had made him lustful. Made him hungry. Made him do things he might not otherwise do. Made him see things he would never have seen.

Like Arella's blood. He saw it in her veins, in the faint pulse at her throat and on her wrist. He felt the vibration of her every heartbeat in the air. He wasn't a vampire. He wasn't driven to consume her blood. But he was a demon. He relished the idea of her bleeding.

He relished other ideas more.

He glanced down into his own lap. It was obvious, some of those ideas. He raised his eyes to hers again.

She never wavered. She smiled. She reached out a hand and touched his leg. They were next to each other on a half-full subway car, but it might as well have been empty. She spoke in the barest whisper. "Everything will be alright."

He shook his head.

"You're not alone in this," she told him.

They didn't take the train all the way up to Grand Central. They got off early, climbed the stairs into Manhattan's early evening. All around them, taxis and buses made their noises, people hurried into shops or down the street.

They abandoned the thickest of the crowds, and at one corner, came into sight of the lot where St. Lazarus' Cathedral once had stood.

He'd seen it before. But it was like seeing it for the first time.

It was an empty spot within the middle of the city. It didn't impact any skyline. It wasn't obvious from certain angles. A block away on most of the roads around it, you might not notice it was missing at all.

But from this direction, which Arella might have chosen intentionally, you could see the shapes of the cathedral in the absences. The negative space filled his eyes and his mind. He saw where there would have been spires. A rose window. He even saw the gargoyles. Sensed their movement. As though they were still alive.

Arella took his hand and squeezed. He had stopped without meaning to. Trying to catch his breath. "Can you see it?" he asked.

"I saw it," Arella told him. "When it was still here. Nene took me once. It had—done a lot to her. For her. She returned regularly until it just wasn't there anymore."

"What happened to it?"

Arella shook her head. "Nobody knows. Or if they know, no one will say. It didn't explode. That would have made the news. No wrecking crew ever came. Just one day, it was gone. A few weeks later, they came and put up the fencing."

Stephen knew all that from his research. It was hard to believe a church made of stone could simply disappear like that. But he also knew what had happened to the gargoyle. It had never been a regular church. Apparently, the gargoyle had been moved during a renovation decades earlier, so that it perched over the doors on the inside of the cathedral, though no one seemed to know why.

Now, there was no gargoyle. It had died.

But there was, again, a demon.

Stephen took a breath, swallowing any hint of trepidation, and strode toward the cathedral. He didn't let go of Arella's hand, though. Did he need the reassurance? Or did he need the audience?

They walked two and a half blocks, the emptiness of the cathedral more palpable with every step. He heard echoes of that long ago conflict, stone grinding on stone as the gargoyle and the murderous demon faced off against each other.

Closer now, so that he could hear footsteps on the hard dirt inside the space of the cathedral, so he could hear racing heartbeats and voices and gravel, he realized those weren't merely memories of the space. They belonged to here and now.

He must've quickened his pace. Arella was forced to run to keep up as he dragged her to the fence.

Was it possible to recognize a heartbeat? It sounded so much like his own.

CHAPTER 14

Pierce looked from side to side, spinning in place, causing a wave of visible agitation to sweep through his congregation. If she wasn't here, directly in front of him, tied down to the altar like she should be, then she must be running.

"Underground," he said, almost a whisper.

The dog's stone ears perked up. The angelic golden woman narrowed her stony eyes. The young girl tightened her grip on the bowl. The other statues flexed their wings, stretched their necks, even sniffed the air.

The statue without features, essentially an unfinished figure straight from somebody's nightmares, took off at a run.

There were ways into the lot. He had climbed up a stairway that twisted up from the subways. The featureless statue made its way in that direction. Pierce followed, as quick as he could, barely seeing it disappear through that open doorway.

He should have sealed the entrances.

He should have at least made sure they were closed.

No, this woman, whoever she was, had come up following his path. How much had she witnessed? What would she tell—and to whom?

Two stone eagles followed the figure down into the subways. They stretched their wings. They moved with utter silence. He didn't know how they did it and, at the moment, he didn't care. They pursued the interloper. The trespasser. The spy.

"Bring her back alive," Pierce called after them. He didn't know if they heard. It didn't matter. If she died, she couldn't reveal his secrets. If she didn't, he didn't have to hunt for his next sacrifice.

The congregation around him was just a beginning. He didn't know how wide a net his spell had thrown, but he would expand it. If he doubled the diameter, that would—the mathematics were beyond him. It would do far more than double the number of his army.

The statue with closed fists around the two eyes turned suddenly. Back toward the insufficient fence. There, again, were eyes. Not green this time. There wasn't light enough to be sure of the color.

The stone angel heard it, too. She turned, and she moved in that direction.

Pierce frowned. He put a hand on the one statue's shoulder, looked down at her closed fists, and said, "Wait. Let the angel take care of this one."

He didn't understand why he was under attack.

Where did they come from? Who sent them? The church? The priest? Not his friend, the priest—but the one he'd seen that night in the cathedral. The priest who'd been here for the fight between the gargoyle and the demon. An avenging priest, a protector clinging to outdated ideals, a remnant of St. Lazarus' Cathedral. A man who should have disappeared with the church but had, instead, been interviewed and photographed after its disappearance.

No, it couldn't be the priest. The priest had essentially ceased to exist years ago. In all his visits to this site, surely Pierce would have come across the man. If he was alive, he had retired to some island nation by now, never to see the snow—or the stone—of New York again.

Others of his congregation scattered, too. He didn't feel like he was losing control so much as his army had mobilized to protect him and his church. And this was most definitely his. This little altar. The heart upon it in all its pieces. The book. Even the eyes.

Only the one statue remained by his side.

She protected the eyes as much as she protected him.

Which was good. He wasn't fit for hand to hand combat with the religious nut jobs shadowing him now. He was, however, equipped to command, and he'd barely had to say a word.

The thing that raced toward Stephen as he peered through a hole in the plywood had no heartbeat. Its feet hitting the ground were more powerful than any heart. It was stone. He didn't know what had happened, but he knew what it was. What it must be.

A gargoyle.

His father had faced a gargoyle inside this church and died.

But his father had been a bad man. Objectively. A murderer. A serial killer, at that, who had collected files on each of his victims. Rick might have begged for an angel to save him, but he had made no effort to save himself.

What was the number? Forty-three. He had been killing those women before he'd begun his transformation. It wasn't the demon that had made him cruel. He had made the demon cruel.

Stephen had a demon inside him, too. He felt a surge of fury ripple through him. He tightened his fists. He barely noticed Arella stepping back and away. This wasn't her fight, though she had brought him here. She couldn't have known. Could she? She had never seen him before today. Even if she had known about him, even if she'd followed every aspect of his life out of some perverse need to know about the demon's family, she could not have directed him to her gallery. That was paranoia. Stephen wasn't a paranoid man.

He also wasn't one to back down from a fight.

Oh, he had made a life of avoiding it. His strength had always been higher, his agility more acute, his resilience noticeable enough that school nurses marveled at his healing.

This gargoyle, running to attack him unprovoked, was a fight he could not avoid.

The demon inside him wanted out.

The gargoyle leapt the fence, throwing all its stone weight into him, enough to crush the bones of anyone else. But Stephen transformed. He allowed the demon to surge through him. To break his bones and stretch his skin. To reform into someone grotesque—he assumed. He hadn't actually seen himself. Certainly, Arella hadn't shied away from him. Okay, maybe not grotesque, but definitely and undoubtedly something beyond human capacities.

So when the gargoyle landed on him, the two crashed backwards. The sidewalk cracked beneath them. As did the gargoyle's stone wings. People on the street suddenly seemed very sparse, scattering in all directions, except Arella who had gone only a few steps.

They rolled on the sidewalk. The gargoyle—was it an angel?—a golden angel?—tried to wrap its stone hands around his shoulders, maybe going for the neck to choke him, but he had grown in an instant. He was bigger than statue had anticipated. Its grip was weak and uncoordinated. Stephen rolled them further, putting the gargoyle on its back, and delivered a series of punches to its face.

Distantly, people screamed. Horns blared. Tires screeched. They were out in the open, a demon and gargoyle fighting in front of countless mobile phones. Strangers recorded him. He felt suddenly shy. He wanted to be anywhere else. His grandfather would see this and he would know. He would banish Stephen.

Lost for a moment in those thoughts, he wasn't prepared for the gargoyle's counterattack. From its back, it thrust a fist at his face. The stone hurt. The stone made him bleed. His head snapped back, briefly, and in that moment the gargoyle impaled his chest with its other hand.

With the fingers of its hand pointed upward, the gargoyle's arm was a blunt spear. It pierced Stephen's skin, cracked his ribs, and broke free on the other side. Agony exploded through him. For a moment, he couldn't see. He couldn't hear anything but his own heart pounding in his ears. Arella might've cried out, but he wouldn't have known. His mother—she was here, wasn't she?—she might have seen it happen, but he didn't know.

Maybe he should have studied fighting, after all, and not shied away from the brute strength he knew he'd one day have.

Blinded by rage, he brought both hands together like an immense sledge hammer and shattered the gargoyle's head beneath him.

Stone pebbles scattered like shrapnel.

He hit the thing that way three or four times before he stopped. He had to stop. He could barely breath, not without immense pain. The stone arm remained inside him. He wrenched himself away, snapping the arm away from the gargoyle's body. He rolled backwards and slammed hard into the fence, causing it to shudder all the way around the entire lot of St. Lazarus'.

He tore the arm from him. It broke into pieces, which he tossed aside in both directions. They were something like marble, painted gold on the outside. He didn't look to make sure he didn't hit Arella. Hadn't even thought about her until it was too late. But that was fine. She wasn't there. He sat alone in a growing pool of blood. The gargoyle was lifeless again, shattered and unmoving. Faces along the street stared. They saw the demon's face, not Stephen's.

Only his grandfather would know it was him.

And maybe his mother. If she was coherent. But she was coherent enough to be here, at St. Lazarus', tonight of all nights. He listened for her heartbeat. He listened for Arella's. He listened for his own.

Two twisted statues, gargoyles perhaps in the shape of circus dwarves, with exaggerated features and thick hands, dragged Arella away. Through darkness, underground, into the heart of the absent cathedral, they grasped her by her shoulders. They pulled her backwards, so that she only saw where they'd been. Their stony grips hurt and maybe damaged her arms. The hard, unforgiving floor scraped her butt and legs. It was too much to struggle against them, so she tried to minimize the damage they might do to her.

They dragged her up a set of stairs into the lights of the empty lot.

They hoisted her off the ground and onto a stone altar.

A man frowned down at her. He was thin, wiry, but towered over her like some sort of spectre. He leaned closer, his breath smelling of death, and asked, "Who sent you?"

ARMY OF BLOOD AND STONE

CHAPTER 15

The world belonged to her now.

She might barely be able to feel the things she touched, but she enjoyed the sound of them when they cracked, broke, and screamed. She reveled in their racing heartbeats. The little gargoyle clung to her, sated, but she wanted more.

They stood atop an apartment building. Others were taller. Office buildings. Luxury high-rises. None of that mattered to her and never had. In life, if there had been a life, in the memories that slipped around the corners of her mind, there had never been anything. No high-rises. No apartments. Nothing bigger than the cathedral—and in this world, that had been removed.

She was nowhere near it now. There, a man existed who had done things to bring mobility back to her. For years, more years than she could count, she hadn't been completely aware of anything. She saw the people, the buildings rising around her, the cars and all their noise. It all existed in the periphery of her dreams. She explored, yes, not just the now but the then. The former. The things she used to know.

There had never been anything she'd loved. Maybe the child. The infant. Clinging then to her breast like the gargoyle now. Silent as flames consumed them.

She hardly remembered it. Didn't try to. But images came to her anyway. Now that she was able to move, she could no longer control the nature of her dreaming. There had been no high-rises then, but there had been cathedrals. She'd lived in the shadow of one. They might not have condemned her directly, but they had done nothing to protect her.

She cooed at the little gargoyle as it rustled. "Sleep, gentle thing," she said, though blood still stained its stony flesh. "Sleep, if you can. But there's more to explore. More to experience. More to understand."

They were no longer connected to the man at the cathedral, but certainly he had expectations of her. Of them. Of the others he had roused. He reminded her — she knew not of what. Something bad. Something ugly.

She wanted to destroy him. Him and his. Everything around him. Not because of the memories he threatened to revive, but because he continued to make that threat. She wanted nothing of her first life. Everything now was new. She was indestructible, a force of nature, and she could do everything different this time.

No one could demean her.

No one could control her.

No one could punish her for imagined sleights.

The baby gargoyle looked up at her and made a sound like a question.

"Yes, little one," she said to it. "We'll have to go back."

The gargoyle asked another question.

"There's nothing else to do," she told the infant.

With that, she dismounted from the rooftop. Returning to the sky, she barely felt the wind against her face, but it was a hint of something. More than anything, she wanted to be able to feel again. Her other senses seemed to work. The salty, coppery taste of fresh blood remained on her tongue and in her belly.

But she felt no weight of the infant gargoyle. She barely felt it against her makeshift flesh. She felt no weight of herself. She had not felt the man's throat at the shore as she'd crushed it. She didn't register the ground beneath her feet. She doubted a man could grab her from behind and she'd even know about it until and unless she inadvertently wrenched his arms from their sockets.

She felt no fear, no anticipation for anything, no worry, and no love.

She had, briefly, felt the tug of the man's control on her, and she'd severed those threads that bound them. But even that had been like mist on her face, simply a thing she was conscious of rather than a true sensation.

If anything, she felt a longing to feel again.

As much as she wanted to destroy the man, the preacher, priest, reviver who meant to control and command her, she wanted to give him an opportunity to finish the job. Restore her ability to feel again. Everything else, she had.

She wanted more.

Chloe retreated into darkness. Into labyrinthine tunnels snaking beneath and between the subways, the water lines and sewage pipes. Streams flowed under the city. Catacombs stretched toward the far reaches of history. The crypts of St. Lazarus had gone with it, but there were many, many others.

And there were vestiges of the past abandoned everywhere.

Tunnels could take her to far reaches of the city, other cities, other states, under the rivers or into forgotten speakeasies maybe occupied by ghosts. Theaters that had closed their doors over a century ago. Churches, little churches, worshipping alternative gods, hid in the crevices left by a haphazard race toward modernization and industrialization.

She understood these things in an offhand kind of way, holding on to the knowledge at the edges of her mind as she slipped through curtains of cobwebs in unseen and unused tunnels. Complete darkness enveloped her. City sounds, subway sounds primarily, but also the hum of wild electricity behind the walls and above the ceilings, the footfalls of a million souls echoing through asphalt and concrete, oriented her.

She should be confused. She was not. She didn't remember a level of clarity so precise, so all-encompassing, as this.

Behind her, monsters mimicked her past. A man, a self-appointed priest, commanded them. Together, they bruised through her own memories, they shattered the few connections she maintained. They had commandeered the cathedral, her St. Lazarus, which had for years stood as a blank reminder of terrors she tried desperately not to remember but needed to keep for herself.

For her son.

Her breath hitched. She caught herself on the brick wall beside her, surprised at how dry it was under her forearm. Sounds of pursuit had dwindled. She was alone, thoroughly alone, breathing air undisturbed since the days of Theodore Roosevelt and George Gershwin. She realized she was panting, desperately, trying to catch her breath, so she paused to give herself the chance.

She had seen things. Stone things. But also flesh. Meat on the altar. Blood. It might have been steak, but she doubted it. She'd eaten steak. It never looked like that. It never reeked like that.

She had heard things. Bring her back alive.

What did he intend to do with her? Rick would never have allowed that. Rick would have come, would have shown him the true face of evil, would have separated his head from his body.

But she had heard something else. Someone else. Outside the fence, someone had been looking in, someone unwanted by the priest wizard necromantic sculptor. Someone else to bring to the altar. To sacrifice. To murder.

She hadn't given it any thought at the moment, not when it took every ounce of her attention and intention just to escape. But she'd registered that intrusion. Why? Why did she care? Because who else would care about what happened in the remnants of a cathedral? It might be the artist. The gargoyle himself returned. Or Rick, Rick's father: the demon revived.

But no, in her hyper-clarity, Chloe knew the only other person in the city who would have any interest in St. Lazarus' Cathedral would be her son. Rick's living and grown son. Little Stephen, not so little anymore, living somewhere in the city, away from her for all these years or decades or maybe forever, in school now, learning things she'd never known, exploring the edges of his world and discovering secrets about himself no one alive, not even his mother, not even Chloe who had given birth to him in an explosion of pain and noise, could help him navigate. Of course he would come back to the source. The sources. He would visit her father, who could tell him stories but actually knew nothing. He could go the warehouse, which had been mostly dismantled and repurposed but which still stood in Brooklyn like a monolith. He could go to his mother, but Chloe had proven, over and over again, that he could not rely on her for anything. So he would come to the cathedral. He would seek the ghosts. The echoes. Remnants of the cathedral's memories.

And he would have found—gargoyles. Lots of little stone gargoyles, the same kinds of thing that had twenty years ago defeated his father and Rick's father.

And she had abandoned him. Again.

She'd caught her breath. She saw faint traces of nothing through the dark. She had gone too far. Too deep. Like one of the monsters, she had dragged herself into hell. She pounded the wall beside her with the butt of her fist, dislodging brick dust. She wiped tears from her eyes. She looked back, toward the gargoyles, the cathedral, her living history.

And she moved.

Her son deserved better. But all he had was her.

CHAPTER 16

Stephen crawled.

He dragged himself away from the cathedral. Over asphalt. Through shadows. In the glare of headlights and the screech of cars and sirens. In the flickering light of dozens of camera phones capturing the essence of a bleeding demon.

Pain shot through him. It radiated from the hole in his chest. Pieces of the golden statue probably remained inside him. Such shrapnel would stay with him forever, biting into him from under his skin, grinding his bones, slicing his veins every time he moved in his sleep or walked or breathed too deeply.

The pain made it difficult to focus. To concentrate. To see clearly. He pulled a grate out of the sidewalk and dropped off the street. Into a basement of some sort. The darkness was not complete. There was no escaping the noises of the city. But for a moment, at least, he might have some privacy. A chance to figure out what had happened. Assess his wounds. Worry about Arella.

He had brought her into this. She was his responsibility.

He crawled into a corner. Crates were stored against the walls and on palettes in the middle of the room, but it was a small room, not much of a basement at all, no doubt attached to something else. It wouldn't take long for someone to find him.

There, in one wall, was a door, and next to it a heavy duty light bulb, currently dark. It would blaze into life. The door would open. People would flood into the room with more cameras. Maybe chains. To take him. To experiment on him. To figure out what made him tick.

He hadn't considered this before.

To the best of his knowledge, there was no one like him anywhere.

His strength was inhuman. How was his healing? The pain burned inside him. He struggled to maintain his demonic form, certain the human version of him would succumb to the wounds.

His father had been a demon, and his father had died at this cathedral.

His father had been a murderer. He'd deserved it. Stephen didn't know what had happened, what had attacked him or why.

With an exhalation, almost a sigh, he gave in and allowed his body to shift. He didn't really have control. He'd fought it as best he could but couldn't resist anymore.

As his body shifted, as the bones rearranged themselves, the skin on his chest started to close. First, it spit out a few splinters of stone that had gotten lodged inside him. They clattered on the floor when they fell. He drew in a breath. It didn't hurt near as much as the last one. Tentatively, he touched his chest. It still bled. The wound had closed some, but not entirely.

Red muscles rippled under the skin of his hand.

He pushed for the transformation. To become, once again, the demon. As long as the cameras saw only the demon's face, not his, Stephen might be able to return to school as if nothing had happened.

He shook his head.

He would never be the same. Especially if something happened to Arella because of him. He released the transformation, becoming once again the demon, and pushed himself to his feet. He used the wall at his back for support, but he didn't really need it now. He could stand. Already, strength surged back through him. The wound looked now like a scar. It was tender, and it hurt, but it wasn't debilitating.

He could worry about the physics, the biology, another time. He looked up at the grate, the opening he'd left, at the face straining to see him in the dark. Before the light had a chance to come on, he bent at the knees and leapt into the air.

He had wings. Something like wings. He didn't have to jump. He could fly. But he didn't know how to fly or how to control himself. He was as graceful as a baby making its first steps. The jump directed him through the opening in the ceiling. He managed to land on the sidewalk. The ground cracked audibly beneath his feet. He took a deep breath, a demonic lungful of air, and turned away from the inquisitive bystanders. With another leap, and the awkward use of those wings, he cleared the fence and landed on the other side.

The lot was occupied by mounds of dirt, piles of rubble, stone walls still standing that may or may not have been part of the original cathedral. There were earth movers, bulldozers, Dumpsters, machines with arms meant to eat at the ground.

And there was an altar.

At the altar, there was a man. A regular normal everyday human, not a demon, not an angel, not a gargoyle. A wiry man who appeared as threatening as an insect. A man with a scowl on his face as he looked up from the altar.

Two stone creatures held Arella down on that altar, one at each arm. Seeing him, she renewed her struggle, but they were stone and heavy and unmoving.

But they were small. As he already knew, stone could be shattered.

The man glanced down at the book in front of him, the only thing separating him from Arella, then looked up again at Stephen and said, "I watched you die."

There were also other gargoyles, stone statues of various shapes and sizes, some not obviously gargoyles at all. They rose from every shadow, stepped from behind every machine and mound.

The one that attacked him was a lion.

It wasn't really a lion. It was a gargoyle with the face of a lion, but a body more akin to the demon's, squat and muscular. It launched itself at Stephen, extending claws, opening its toothy mouth wide. Once upon a time, maybe, it had stood at the highest height of the cathedral, one of the original gargoyles that had somehow persisted beyond its disappearance.

Stephen dropped back into something of a defensive stance. He hadn't realized there was one closer to him, low on the ground. The snake-like dragon thing wrapped itself around his legs, pulling them together, throwing him off-balance before the lion struck.

It struck hard.

The three of them tumbled backwards.

He got a hand on the lion's throat. There was nothing to squeeze. He flexed his legs, but for the moment they were bound tight.

The man, the priest, spoke calmly from the altar. He spoke to Arella, but Stephen heard him clearly. "You brought back the demon. Or the demon brought you. You must be special. I don't know how. It would be better if I knew, but that doesn't matter. You blood will be better."

Stephen ignored the lion and the snake and the other statues piling on top of him and stared instead at the long, black blade in the priest's hand as he lifted it overhead. His eyes were half closed, his other hand pointed at words in the book, his whispers too soft and too foreign for Stephen to make out the words.

Calling upon every reserve of strength, on the essence of his father and grandfather and all other demons before him, Stephen flailed at the statues holding him down. He crushed one, shattered another, dislodged the lion for a moment. But a dozen others crawled over him, pulling at each of his limbs, holding him down and preventing him from moving.

He tried to say something, but he had no words. He didn't have strength enough to free himself in time to stop that knife from descending.

Stephen pushed up anyway. He flung the smaller statues aside. He brought down a heavy clawed fist on the snake's dragon head. A scream escaped him, an amalgamation of fury and frustration. He used everything he had in him, every muscle, every fear, every legend he'd ever read about. He called upon the power of gods, thunder gods and war gods, gods of love and gods of strength. He drew upon whatever essence of St. Lazarus remained on this site. The priest paused a moment to look at Stephen. The gargoyles holding Arella down looked at him.

He bucked two of the gargoyles like a horse. He wriggled and writhed. And he managed to raise his back off the ground as the priest brought the blade down at Arella's chest.

Stephen cried out. But someone else, someone in the shadows, someone he almost didn't recognize, emerged from the darkness and struck the priest from behind. He fell forward, crashing down on top of Arella. The knife clattered impotently away.

A moment later, the sky crackled with thunder and a torrent of rain poured down.

CHAPTER 17

At first, Chloe stopped herself. She'd returned, and what she saw terrified her. The priest with his sacrifice. And her son—Stephen—in full demonic form. He looked so much like his father, it stopped Chloe dead in her tracks. He was on the ground, being overwhelmed by an army of gargoyles. But it was clear he intended to stop the priest and prevent the sacrifice.

So Chloe, who knew she's never been much of a mother, and had no hope of ever being much more of a mother, in this moment could be exactly the mother he needed. She lashed out at the priest just as he raised the black-bladed knife. Just before he spilled the blood.

She spilled his.

She picked up a chunk of rock, maybe concrete, maybe granite, maybe a remnant of the gargoyle who had been here twenty years before. The pieces of this cathedral stretched back in time. They connected her to Rick. They connected Stephen to his father.

But this time, Stephen was no murderer facing some twisted yet righteous justice. He was her son.

She wasn't going to let him fail.

So she struck the priest with a piece of the disappeared cathedral.

She struck low. Maybe the brick was too heavy to life as high as she'd expected. She aimed for the head, but hit the priest just below the back of his neck. It didn't shatter his skull, but it threw him forward. It loosened his grip on the knife.

It did nothing to the gargoyles holding down the sacrifice.

He fell forward, over her, with a kind of whimper.

At that moment, perhaps pulling strength from her, Chloe's demon son cast aside the gargoyles on top of him. He rose to his feet. He smashed one of the statues with a closed fist. Stone shattered. He hit another hard enough to throw it backwards and off its feet.

The priest was already regaining himself. He hadn't gotten entirely upright, but rolled first to the side so he could grab that knife.

He snarled as the demon approached him.

More gargoyles rose from behind Chloe. They were eagles. Distorted representations of something like eagles. They raced forward, toward Stephen, talons extended to do maximum damage.

He didn't seem to see them.

He was focused on the priest and the things holding the woman to the altar.

Chloe called his name. A warning. A plea. She only needed him to adjust what he was looking at by a little bit and he would see what came for him.

He turned, but it was too late. The first eagle hit him in the face. Because he'd turned, it wasn't a direct hit, but it was still solid. Bone and stone cracked. He ripped that first eagle from the air and, with a scream, slammed it to the ground, breaking it into a thousand pieces.

The second eagle hit his bleeding face directly.

Stephen stumbled backwards. He flailed, trying to catch the second eagle, but went down on his back.

The priest grinned as he returned to his feet. He didn't even glance in Chloe's direction. He knew the gargoyles protected him. They answered to him. Obeyed him. They had been dying for him in front of this deranged altar.

Chloe hit him again. The second blow didn't have

the power or effect of the first. He turned. He slashed at her with the knife. The blade cut fast and drew blood. She fell back, dropping her bludgeon, dropping all pretense that she could help in a battle of gargoyles and demons. Hers was a body of flesh, weak and fragile, unable to stand up against any onslaught. It would take the rest of her life to catch her breath. She might never draw another one.

The priest slashed at her again, but she was already on the ground. On her back. Red hot pain screaming in her chest and rippling through her body.

The priest, apparently satisfied, turned to face Stephen instead.

And there he was: her son, the son of the demon she'd loved, her child whom she'd carried for most of nine months, a massive conglomeration of bulging muscles, bleeding now and bruised, maybe broken, maybe damaged beyond repair. Her son, who had come on his own to this cathedral, seeking answers about his future from the things and places adjacent to his past. Her son, who had tried to save this woman, this woman who was Chloe's age, possibly a mother herself, maybe even a surrogate mother for her son because she'd been so damned bad at it. Her son, the demon, standing in a field of stone rubble. Standing and snarling. Growling. Showing all of what he'd inherited from his father.

"Destroy him," the priest said, almost under his breath, to any and all of the statues that remained.

The two gargoyles holding down his intended sacrifice leapt at the demon. The woman, released, shot up into a sitting position. The priest didn't look at her. It wasn't much of a distance, but she launched herself through the air and crashed into the priest from behind.

They went down.

Stephen and the remaining gargoyles, maybe six or seven of them, went down.

Chloe felt her life draining. The blood flowed hotly from her. She laid back and closed her eyes and wished for the noise of everything to go away.

But that would mean death.

And she wasn't prepared to die.

She opened her eyes in time to see the priest running away.

In time to see her son forced to one knee as he defended himself against absurd stone creatures.

In time to see darkness creep in on the world from all the corners of her vision.

She tried to push herself up off her back, but there was too much pain.

The other woman was at her side now, kneeling there, holding her hand and looking down at the wound. Chloe couldn't look at it. She didn't think she could look at it on someone else. She'd always wanted the vampire's life, or death, but she didn't know if she could handle the blood. Feasting on it. Drowning in it.

The woman said something to her, something meant to be soothing, her voice a calm and hushed whisper in the middle of every other sound of New York City.

Chloe shook her head. She managed to say, "I'm doomed," then leaned her head back again to close her eyes.

"What?" the woman asked. "No, you're fine, you're gonna be fine. Keep your eyes open. Look at me. Look at me."

Chloe did as she was told. How could you ignore that kind of authority?

"You're going to be fine," the woman told her. "Where does it hurt?"

"He cut me," Chloe said.

The woman frowned at her. "Did you hit your head?"

"No."

"Did you black out?"

"No."

"Did you lose consciousness at all?"

Chloe hesitated. "I want to."

The woman nodded. She understood. She maybe had the same vices and experiences. She seemed unconcerned by the demon, the gargoyles, even the priest who had meant to bury a black blade in her chest. "You're right," she said. "He cut you. It's—more of a scratch, if you ask me."

"But the blood."

The woman shook her head.

Behind her, Stephen limped into view. His face was a mess of angry red bruises. Blood dripped from his nose and other wounds. One eye had swollen so much, she couldn't see if it was open or closed or entirely missing. He wasn't the demon anymore. He was human. Frail like his mother. Damaged. Broken.

ARMY OF BLOOD AND STONE

CHAPTER 18

Arella stared down at the woman for a while. She'd closed her eyes and clutched her midsection as though she'd been gouged open by a maddened bull. The woman wasn't unconscious and wasn't pretending to be, but she was doing her best to block out everything else in the world. Rain fell without impact on her face.

The woman. Arella knew who she was.

Stephen's mother.

He limped toward her. Knelt beside her. His face was all questions. His voice was only a tremor, not an actual word, but the sound cut through the aftermath of what had just happened.

Arella's heart raced.

The priest had gone away. The statues that had helped him, living gargoyles and the like, were either destroyed or gone, probably with him. She didn't give any time to thinking of where they might have gone or where they might have come from. She'd gotten in bed—literally—with a demon. The rest of this was now inevitable.

It wasn't midnight yet. It wasn't even close.

Stephen looked up from his mother. He hadn't touched her, not yet. That might mean all sorts of things. Arella tried not to read anything into it. She understood enough. "Who was that?"

Arella shook her head.

"That," his mother said without opening her eyes and without turning her head, "was an echo of the past."

He looked down at her. Her existence, and her blood, had him more defeated than anything else Arella had seen tonight. He said, "Not my past."

"Our past," his mother said, shaking her head. "Our past is—inescapable. I thought you could escape it, but you couldn't. Because of you, because of what you are, what Rick was—because of all that, there are gargoyles."

Arella looked around, away from the demon and his mother. She didn't need to be told who Rick was. She knew. She even knew the name. Nene Spirito had told her a lot. She'd read the papers back then. She might even have a few in a box tucked in the deepest corner of her closet. She'd loved Nene, and had listened to every tale the woman had spun. She'd collected the proofs, and the refutations, and the inaccuracies. She found it hard to believe a demon had hunted the streets of New York City, but she'd never really doubted Nene.

Had she?

And now, Arella knew for certain. She'd seen it with her own eyes. Felt it with her own body. She knew why Nene had fixated on the subjects she'd chosen, the church and the gargoyle, and the ghost, only sometimes the demon but usually in the background.

She had texted Nene earlier but gotten no response. The artist was living her best life somewhere in Florida, away from reminders of what must've been some of the hardest days of her life. She'd painted with fervor for a while, she'd created amazing, thickly textured images with horsehair and oils. She'd thrown all of herself into it—or so Arella had thought. But she hadn't been trying to capture anything. She'd been trying to purge.

Arella looked around for any signs that the priest or his brood had returned. A mere step or two took her back to the altar. She put a finger on the pages of the open book.

"No," Stephen said. So much time had passed, Arella almost forgot they were talking behind her. She turned. Stephen's mother had opened her eyes and turned her head at that.

"What do you mean, no?" she asked. "I'm still your mother."

"You," Stephen said, "abandoned me."

She shook her head. "I couldn't. I couldn't. My father, he insisted—you needed—you needed not me."

"What I needed," Stephen said, "was foreknowledge."

His mother smiled. Still laying there, she looked down at her body. "I can't see my organs." She touched the blood on her shirt. "He cut me."

"I needed to know what to expect," Stephen said. "How to prepare."

She shook her head again. Violently. In passionate denial. "I don't know how you prepare. I don't know what to expect. I only know—you have your father in you."

"You knew what he was," Stephen said. "Even then."

"Maybe then. But I didn't really know. I couldn't. I wasn't there for it. I mean, I saw it, I witnessed it, I was there when he—when he became what he was. What you are. But I didn't and don't know how it worked. How he did it. I always thought—I wanted him to make me into what he was. Like a vampire." She laid her head back. A soft smile crept over her face. "We would've lived forever. Together. But—but—that gargoyle killed him. These gargoyles, they came to finish the job. To end his line. You, Stephen." She closed her eyes. "You look so much like him."

"Grandpa warned me," Stephen said. "You should've..." His words faltered. He looked up, at Arella, as though she might have better answers for him.

"I should've a lot of things," his mother said. "But I didn't. I couldn't. I can't. I just can't. Give me a minute. I can't think. I can't see. I don't know what's going on. I don't know how they're here, but I know why. To finish what they started."

Arella shook her head and said, "No."

She wasn't sure Stephen's mother heard her.

"No," she said again. "Nene told me what happened. She told me all about it. She sketched it a thousand times. Painted it dozens of times. It never left her. She never escaped it. And she never, not once, said anything about a man commanding the gargoyle."

"Not a man. A priest."

"Not a real priest," Arella said. "Not a priest of the church. And there had only been one gargoyle then. One. She'd told me. She thought they were both going to die." She closed her eyes. She felt everything Nene had felt back then, though none of this was her story. "She said he was her redemption. And she was his."

"What does that mean?" Stephen asked.

"This is not that story, continued," Arella said. "That gargoyle is gone."

"There was a priest then, too."

Stephen looked down at his mom. "He's gone. He disappeared after the cathedral."

Arella snapped shut the book on the altar and said, "We shouldn't stay here."

From outside the cathedral's abandoned lot, she heard sirens, people talking, people sobbing. What might have happened on the outside of the fence while they were struggling on the inside? But there were authorities here now, and those flashing lights reached into the lot of St. Lazarus'.

"Unless you want to explain who and what you are," Arella said.

Stephen's mother pushed herself into a sitting position. She looked at Arella for what might have been the first real time, then turned to Stephen. "Who is she?"

"She's helping me," Stephen said.

"You can't lie to me."

"Chloe," he said, emphasizing her name with an unkind harshness, accentuating that he wasn't calling her Mom. He softened his voice to add, "I'm not the one telling lies."

"Fine," she said. "We'll hide, then. Like cowards. I know where to go."

———

Chloe led them down into darkness and shadow. Her head felt clear, but there was too much, too much volume and too much noise, too many things going on all at the same time. She needed the silence they would find in the dark.

But what she really needed was serenity.

Silence never brought peace. It made the voices inside her that much louder. What she really needed was a heavy driving beat she could throw herself into and pills that would separate her from her body. She fought that urge. She couldn't be any good to her son in that condition. She wasn't any good to him in this condition. Honestly, she wasn't any good at all.

But she had to try.

Had she failed Rick? She hadn't been given the chance. Somehow, she'd failed him without knowing she ever had the chance. If she failed Stephen, she would do so with her eyes open.

Instinct and memory guided her through the dark. They passed away from the tunnels and corridors known to modern commuters and slipped into a part of the city forgotten, hidden, and lost.

A part of the city that was just like her.

The other woman, Stephen's friend, had known Nene Spirito. That fact filled Chloe's head with so much noise. She could see the artist clearly in her mind, though she wasn't sure if she'd ever encountered her in real life or only her picture in newspapers and magazines. She'd been there to watch Rick die.

Chloe hadn't seen that. She'd been denied that particular privilege. She'd been denied so many privileges when it came to Rick. She missed him. Terribly. Completely. It was hard to escape the memory of the most amazing, exciting, and dangerous man she'd ever known.

She wiped tears from her eyes but said nothing — just led them deeper into the underground night, and finally to a door that needed muscle to open. She touched it, lowered her head, then stepped aside. "Stephen," she said. "Please."

It wasn't much of a door. It was some sort of metal, old and covered with mold, rust, webbing, and it hadn't been opened in maybe a century. But Chloe knew what was behind that door. And she knew only someone like Rick, with that kind of inhuman strength, would be able to get through it. She'd tried two or three times in the past. She didn't even bother now.

Stephen limped forward. He was hurt. She'd forgotten that. He'd been badly hurt, and here she was making him show off his strength like a child in a circus.

She saw the strain in his muscles as he grasped the curved handle and pulled the door. At first, nothing happened. The door refused to move. Probably frozen in place.

Stephen said, "It's locked."

"Then break it," Chloe said. "You're stronger than you know, Stephen."

He sighed. He said, "Step back." He motioned Chloe and his friend aside. A wave of distortion passed under his skin. As he transformed, where the noise of the city was less and while Chloe's head was mercifully hushed, she heard the individual muscles inside him snap. His bones cracked. He tore himself apart from the inside out and became the demon, stitching himself back together in better condition than he'd been in, and he tugged on the door.

The locking mechanism, a hundred years old, might've been tough then and even now, but it couldn't resist a demon's power. Metal bent and shattered, the lock died a horrible death, and the door opened onto a speakeasy.

CHAPTER 19

The baby fussed.

She held it firmly. Not too tight, though. She didn't know the limits of her strength or the baby's. The gargoyle nestled into her and mewled and stretched out its little hand. Opening and closing fingers.

It inspired a vague and distant memory.

She stood in her spot. Where she had been for longer than her awareness. She watched the site of the cathedral. She had seen it, she was sure she had, though maybe it had only been the ghost of the cathedral. Certainly, she had never seen the gargoyle.

But she knew about it.

And now, she knew about the demon.

Oh, she hadn't expected to see that. A glorious spectacle of stone and flesh. If she could have shivers in her spine, this would have given them to her.

The demon disguised itself as a man. She liked that. She wondered if she could do something about her appearance. Anyone, upon seeing her, would know pretty quickly she wasn't human. She had no flesh. No eyes. There was nothing soft or supple about her. Nothing fragile like bones.

A void existed inside her. The void swallowed everything. Her past. Her memories. The life she'd lived before. She saw brief images. She might even have known the places. Did she remember her name? No. No, she did not. She didn't need it. It tied her to a history that wasn't hers anymore. That world was gone, replaced with automobiles and computers and constant blinking, bleeping, and bruising. The world had grown harsh and brutal. She had been singled out. Made to suffer. Her and her child.

The gargoyle jostled for a better fit against her. "There, there," she whispered.

The world she'd lived in had destroyed her in a very real way. Here she was in a new world, immune to the dangers around her, her skin and emotions both impermeable. She felt nothing. She knew nothing. She was—nothing.

If she had any sense of smell, she would've chased after the priest. The man who controlled the threads that connected those lesser statues to him. The puppeteer. Marionettist.

He knew things.

But the things he knew had been written in that book, and that book had been taken by one of the women.

So when they slipped off the surface of the city, she sighed. And she followed them.

She didn't need light to see. But she couldn't squeeze herself, especially carrying the baby gargoyle, into tighter spaces, either. She got only so far, then could go no more.

The gargoyle reached forward, into the dark, with its little hands.

"Can you follow them?" she asked, keeping her gravel voice quiet. She wasn't sure the words reached the gargoyle, but it seemed to understand. "Find where they go, then find a way to the surface so I can follow after them."

The gargoyle looked up at her. Its stony eyes met hers. She felt something like an emotion then. They'd slaughtered her, so many years ago, and her baby with her. The world had always been cruel. Was she being given another chance?

Not without that book.

"Go," she said to the gargoyle.

Did it smile? Could a little gargoyle with crude features like that express any sort of emotion? Did it feel emotions?

She understood the concept of jealousy. It had never applied in her previous life or in her dreams. Now, it was the thing she most felt. Jealousy at the fact that everyone and everything around her could feel anything other than jealousy and empty longing and some degree of anger.

And hunger.

She had fed the baby. She hadn't fed since dawn.

"Do this for me," she said to the gargoyle.

And it said, as best it could, "Mama."

If she'd had a heart, it would've skipped a beat then. Maybe two. She had severed the threads that bound the gargoyle to everything and everyone but her. They were united. Inseparable.

The gargoyle pushed out of her arms. It didn't drop to the ground. It flew further into the darkness in a shroud of absolute stealth.

They would have to find each other again.

She knew they would.

In the meantime, she had to deal with her hunger. She didn't have a stomach, or any internal organs to speak of. What she needed might be purely metaphorical. But the gargoyle had absorbed the spilled blood of a random man in an alley. She had done so on the shore of Coney Island, unaware that she was doing it and unaware she even needed anything.

She moved with an easy silence. She crept into the darkness, not away from the sounds of people but toward them. She didn't want a crowd. Attention of any sort would prevent her from regaining the one thing she wanted. More than sustenance, she wanted and needed to breathe again. To feel the ground beneath her feet. The chill on the air.

Her sense of hearing was sublime. She could track a person by their heartbeat, their breathing, the pulse of blood in their veins. She didn't know the history of New York's underground. She didn't know anything of its twists and turns. When she soared, in her mind, as she had done for years before the priest had gifted her once again with motion, she had kept to the streets and the skies. Trying to make sense of the labyrinth only confused her.

But she didn't need to know her away around in order to locate prey. A man alone and isolated. He laid under a tattered coat in a hidden corner. He watched the shadows and mumbled to himself and clutched something in his gloved hand. He kept it close to his chest. The gloves were incomplete, missing a few fingers, with holes and dirt in the wool. He wore a ski cap over his head. It came down over his eyebrows but not his eyes. Those were hazy, muted, and weak.

When finally he saw her, he said, "Ana?"

She said nothing.

"Is that you?" he asked. His voice was gruff and broken. He glanced down at the thing, a printed photograph, in his hand. It was small. He held it like a treasure.

"I always hoped you'd come back," he said. He paused, glanced from side to side, then looked straight at her. "You were right. You were always right. I was never good at thinking. I thought we were immortal, Ana. I thought we could do anything and survive anything."

He glanced down at the photograph. His lip trembled. Moisture rolled out of one of his eyes. "They told me you were dead," he said.

She moved closer.

"You're not here to forgive me," he said. "It's time. It's my time. I'm ready. I pray that you're here to claim me and not condemn me."

She paused. She stood over him now, staring down, and hesitated. He meant nothing to her. He wasn't anyone. Condemnation, though—she wasn't here for that. She'd experienced it herself. She and her baby. Long ago. She didn't mean to become the executioner.

She would've sighed between realizations. She wasn't here to execute or condemn. She was here because of a need inside her. She knelt, straddling him, knees on either side of his hips.

He held up the photograph.

She set her hand upon his chest. Where he had held the picture. Underneath, there was a heart doing its best to keep him alive. She pressed down, tearing through flesh and splintering bone. She did it fast. He made a sound. Blood oozed from his mouth. She bent over to taste it. There was no taste, but she tried to be gentle. A final kiss for the dying. This was a mercy.

Her lips absorbed the blood. So did her hand in his chest.

It was a slow process. Eventually, he ceased crying. No fresh tears and no fresh blood spilled from him. It was on her now, a good amount of it, on her mouth, her hands and knees. It quelled part of the emptiness. It satiated her baser needs.

Gingerly, she took the photograph from his hand. A face stared back at her. A woman with raven hair. She'd had raven hair, herself. She remembered that now.

She'd looked exactly like this woman once. Dark hair and dark eyes didn't mean a dark heart, but she'd been condemned anyway.

Maybe she'd been guilty.

She had no memory of guilt. Maybe she'd been guilty then of something she wouldn't do until reviving in this future time and faraway place. Maybe she'd only been guilty of anything because of the punishment.

She left what remained of him and made her way back to the streets. She listened for the sounds of rain. Rain would wash her clean. She would wear, again, the face of an angel.

CHAPTER 20

Pierce fled the cathedral.

Everything had gone wrong. He'd lost the book. He'd lost half his army.

But—there was a bright side—he'd drawn blood.

In flickering incandescent lights deep beneath the city, he paused. He looked down at his ceremonial blade. Sure, he had wanted to spill much more blood than this, but he had succeeded. He had cut that woman. Her blood stained the blade, and it had fallen onto the altar, over the heart, over the remnants of the spell casting he'd done.

He thrust the blade into its sheath and stashed it in his jacket's inner pocket. He pulled out his cell phone, but this deep below the surface, separated from actual subway lines by too much brick, too much concrete, too many ancient water and electrical lines, it found no signal. The weight of history pressed down on him.

He had seen so much of it. Survived so much.

Now, Pierce needed to create a bit of his own.

But the demon! He took a breath, tried to make sense of it. Had he brought forth another demon by bringing life to stone? Was it a side effect of the same spell? Did the existence of one automatically require existence of the other?

Then the demon should have been in thrall to him no less so than the statues.

He frowned. He moved through the dark until he reached crowded tiled walls. There, keeping away from others, he dialed a number. The signal was weak. The phone rang. He climbed steps to get higher, closer to the surface.

His priest answered without a word.

"Forgive me, Father," Pierce said.

"I'm watching the news," the priest told him. His voice, deep as it was, sounded distant, physically and emotionally. "I'm seeing things I shouldn't be seeing, Pierce."

"I don't know what you're seeing," Pierce said.

"Tell me what happened."

Pierce took a breath. He'd been out of contact with his friend. He knew the inequities in their relationship. Friend wasn't the right word. He had thought he might correct that. Instead, he said, "It worked."

There was a brief moment of silence between them. But instead of expressing surprise, the priest said, "The world knows."

"What does the world know?" Pierce asked.

"Forget the world," the priest told him. "Think of your soul, Pierce—friend—and absolve yourself. Give me the details."

"I revived the statue," Pierce said. "And...others."

"More than just the one?"

"A dozen, at least."

"What else?"

"A—I think it's a demon," Pierce said.

He reached the street, far enough from the cathedral that he couldn't see it, couldn't hear any of what might be happening there over the sounds of everything else happening throughout the city. New York was never quiet and never still.

The priest paused a moment, then said, "I suspected."

"The gargoyles—might have destroyed it, might have been destroyed, but..." He paused. He didn't know if he wanted to go further, but the priest wasn't ready to leave what he'd just said.

"You don't know?"

"I had to run."

"You ran?"

"The demon wasn't alone. The next sacrifice— maybe she had friends. I didn't think she would. She looked lost to me." The priest remained quiet to let him continue. "I managed to spill her blood. To complete the spell again. She probably isn't dead—but I doubt anyone would believe what she tells them."

"What do you mean, you completed the spell again?"

"I broadened its reach," Pierce said. "To animate more." He didn't say, to build my army, but that was exactly what he'd intended. Not the priest's army. This wasn't merely some experiment.

He had met the priest outside the cathedral's grounds shortly after it had disappeared. The priest had known Father O'Leary, had known the stories, had listened to Pierce without judgement and offered— salvation? No. Redemption. He'd spun his own version of what had happened, a war between good and evil that had been fought for centuries. This was merely a skirmish over the soul of a single woman, an artist haunted by her own failings. And he had told the priest his own story, almost all that he had seen that night.

And now, Pierce knew, they were arriving at the culmination of their story.

More gargoyles.

More demons.

"Well," the priest said, breaking the stretching silence, "it looks like I'm going to have to meet this demon myself."

"What?"

"Clearly, you're the wrong kind of coward for what must come next," the priest said. He disconnected.

Pierce ducked into an alcove, out of the pedestrian traffic. He slipped the phone back into his pocket, worked to control his breathing, then walked to the intersection. He ignored the people, the voices, and distant sirens until he reached the corner and could see the space in which the cathedral had been.

The emptiness of it was overwhelming.

There, the crowds thickened. Even in New York, it was noticeable. Pierce stood for a moment to take in the entirety of what he saw. The spires that had been there, the rose window—all of that remained fresh in his vision. Part of the fence had been opened, presumably by the police that had that section cordoned off. Inside, he had his own altar, and that book—unless the woman and her demon had taken it. He had work still to do. Especially if his friend, the priest, was coming.

⸻

The police would find the shattered remains of a half dozen gargoyles. Those would mean nothing to the cops, to any authority, but they meant everything to Pierce. They'd been loyal. They'd been proof of concept.

But they would also find a human heart. Maybe eyes. He didn't know if the tall statue keeping those eyes—one blue, one hazel—had survived the demon. He didn't even know if it had stayed. It might still be on site, still as a statue, hands closed around its treasures, just a part of the background as far as anyone else would know.

But the heart was definite. Sliced into pieces as it was, they might not immediately recognize it for what it was, but they would know it was something that needed to be bagged, tagged, and examined.

His fingerprints were all over the scene. Rain might wash them away.

He didn't care. They had no prior record of him. He'd never been arrested. As far as he knew, his prints had never been taken for any reason. No database would reveal any of his names. Those would not help them find him.

It wouldn't matter.

He looked to the sky, to the skyline and the rain, to places where other statues might begin to appear. His army was out there. As if they were connected to him, he felt them out there. Coming slowly to life. Emerging into this world ready to obey their creator.

Not the priest.

They would obey him.

Pierce allowed himself to smile. He didn't care how it might look to anyone else. No one was paying him any attention. People were barely paying any attention to the police, either. Such a jaded city. Those who stayed to watch had probably already seen something they couldn't explain, but not a single one of them had seen Pierce.

He looked around the crowds. He followed his intuition.

And there, he started to see things. One of the stone eagles had survived. They'd always been twisted and deformed. It perched on the edge of a roof across the street from the cathedral and seemed to look straight at him.

Nearer, the dog sat on the outside of a subway entry. The dog stared at the cathedral. It didn't move, didn't wag its tail, and seemed to escape everyone else's notice.

In the shadows, other things moved. Shapes. Figures. Statues he hadn't seen earlier.

A stone man stood in the nearby alley, feathers on his helmet and at his ankles, a not-quite full size rendition of Hermes, the Greek messenger god. An iron dragon no bigger than the dog. A woman without arms. A man with a sword. An abstract shape that defied easy explanation or description. They gathered around the edges of Pierce's perception, in shadows and out of sight, but connected to him and making themselves known.

And there were others.

He had, quite possibly, awakened a city's worth of statuary.

CHAPTER 21

A layer of grime coated every surface of the speakeasy. Even the brick walls looked covered in it where they weren't crumbling to dust. Stools were connected to the bar by spider webs. The bar itself had been stripped of any glory so all that remained was a bare wood top and plenty of stains.

Against one wall, there was a decaying upright piano.

There were also booths. Any cushions on those seats had long since disintegrated. Chairs stood around a handful of scattered high tables, but nothing looked strong enough to rest weary bones upon.

Still, Chloe plopped herself in one.

Stephen stared at her. For a while. She leaned back and closed her eyes and held a hand pressed to the wound on her chest. Arella, meanwhile, explored the area, walking behind the bar to the cash register, an ancient machine with round buttons and an open, empty till. There were glasses, but the glass shelves which once upon a time had held bottles of whiskey and tequila were empty except for cracks and smudges in the barely functional mirror behind them. Some of the bricks were discolored where perhaps paintings had once hung.

Arella found a bottle of something under the counter. She set it on the warped wood of the bar. For a moment, Chloe eyed it, but it didn't take long for her to realize the liquid inside had become a breeding ground for things small, crawling, and unmentionable.

"This is amazing," Chloe said, breathless, leaning back again so she could stare at one of several mostly-intact chandeliers. She reached up, as if seeing stars in its old lightbulbs.

"What is this place?" Stephen asked.

"A reprieve," Chloe said. "A sanctuary."

"A bar," Arella added.

Chloe didn't look at Stephen. She kept her eyes toward the sky as though she might see it through layers of New York City's underground. Stephen had no idea what might be above them. She said to him, "You have to heal yourself."

"It's slow," Stephen said.

Chloe shook her head. "It's not that slow. Shift. Become like your father. You will heal."

Stephen shook his head. "I've healed some," he said. "Not completely."

"That's amazing," Arella said, staring at him in awe. He didn't like the way she looked at him now. Earlier, there had been something between them, but now she looked with the eye of a scientist. An explorer on the verge of discovery.

"It hurts," Stephen said. "A lot."

"Transform," Chloe said.

"That's what hurts," Stephen told her.

"Where have you been?" Arella suddenly asked his mother. "When he needed you, you ran away. You disappeared. You took all the secrets of his nature, of his father, and buried them inside yourself."

Chloe popped out of the chair. She stood to face the other woman, but after a moment of locking eyes, bowed her head. "I can't," she said. "I can't remember, I can't keep track, I can't hold onto anything. I was never fit to be a mother."

"But you were a mother," Arella said, stepping out from behind the bar.

"You couldn't have done better. Not with the things I knew. Not with what I saw."

"He's here, now, you know." Arella pointed at Stephen. "Your son. Your demon son, if that's what you want to call the thing inside him. He's here now and needs your help. He needs your knowledge."

"He needs a mother's love," Chloe said. "I was never able to give that."

"Enough," Stephen said.

Both women looked at him, their next words tumbling away.

"Enough," Stephen said again, not so sharply. "What do we do now?"

"What do you mean?" Chloe asked.

"That man tried to kill you," Stephen said. "And he had an army of statues at his side."

Chloe narrowed her eyes. "I still don't know who she is. Isn't she a little old to be your girlfriend?"

Arella slapped her.

"Stop," Stephen said, stepping between them. He looked at his mother. "She's a friend. She's a friend of mine, and she was a friend of the artist."

Chloe hesitated. "The artist? The one in the cathedral that night? The one seeing ghosts?"

"That's the one," Arella said.

"Yeah, well, she would know something useful, wouldn't she?" Chloe said. "What can you do?"

"I suggested the cathedral, "Arella said. "Where we, if I need to remind you, found you."

"We almost all died," Chloe said.

"None of us did."

She lifted her hand from her chest to show the fresh blood. The wound wasn't still bleeding. Her shirt hid it well enough that Stephen couldn't see if it was deep.

She said, "He still got my blood."

"What does that mean?" Arella asked. She looked at Stephen. "Do you know?"

"It means nothing," Stephen said. "It means he didn't kill my mom."

Chloe shook her head. "It means he did his spell. I saw that book. I heard what he was saying. Those were ancient words. Foreign words. Not just another language, but another dimension of language."

"What does that even mean?" Stephen asked.

Chloe said sat back down with a sigh "He'll have more gargoyles the next time we see him."

"More?" Arella asked.

"He created them," Chloe said. She looked up at Stephen. "But he didn't create you. He cannot control you. You can stop him."

"Stop him from doing what?" Stephen asked.

She looked away and didn't answer, but she shook her head and tears were slipping from her eyes.

"From killing more," Arella answered for her.

"I'm not a hero," Stephen said. "I don't even know how to control this—this—whatever this is."

A sound in the darkness got all their attention. The dark of the speakeasy hid shadows. The shadows obscured the gloom. The only light in the speakeasy was what fell through cracks in the ceiling and wall, which hardly provided any.

But the sound was something moving. Almost scurrying. Another day, Stephen might assume it was a rat. It was, after all, New York City, and they were deep underground. But considering everything that had already happened, and all that might still happen, he knew better. He narrowed his eyes even as his body transformed.

Pain rippled through him, though maybe it healed some of his more dangerous wounds. His bones cracked, his muscles stretched, and his vision sharpened.

He saw, in a corner near the door they'd come through, a hole in the ceiling where maybe there had once been vents or pipes or anything else. Now, there was a statue, one of the gargoyles that had chased after them.

If there was one, there might be more. One might have even gone back to alert the man, the priest, whatever he was.

The gargoyle was small. It didn't seem to have teeth, or even claws, but it had wings. It rose, without more sound, toward a crevice in the ceiling. It might lead anywhere. Stephen didn't know and he didn't care. He was taller now, and quicker. He reached after it, swatting the thing from the air. It crashed into the wall of the fissure before it could disappear, then dropped like a stone to the ground.

The thing staggered to its feet. He'd broken one of the wings, so when it tried to rise into the air again, it flew crooked. The thing's face was deformed, its eyes too close, its nose crushed, its ears virtually non-existent. But it had a mouth, misshapen though it was. And it had stone hands, not claws or talons. It pounded on Stephen's fist as he closed it around stone. When he squeezed, he ground stone under his fingers.

Chloe, behind him, groaned at the sound.

He said to the little winged man, "Talk to me, or there will be nothing left of you but crumbs."

ARMY OF BLOOD AND STONE

CHAPTER 22

Her son reminded her so much of his father. Rick had been brash, relentless, and unwilling to compromise. The way Stephen grabbed that little gargoyle, the way he threatened to grind it into nothing, brought back so many images of Rick.

The way he sometimes ground her bones into dust.

His mouth. His rage.

Chloe's breath caught in her throat. For a long time, before he'd died and after, she thought she had loved Rick. Loved him with all her heart. Now, seeing echoes of him in her son, seeing the legacy he'd passed down into this world, a surge of fear struck her.

She tried to back away, but where could she go?

She had spent all her life running away. From the voices. From her emotions. From the things she saw in this world. Indecency. Cruelty.

She was going to be sick. Every pill, every drink, every breath of smoke threatened to tear her apart, and the grinding of stone exasperated it. She didn't feel in control of herself anymore. The wound in her chest— from the priest at the site of the cathedral—burned. It reminded her of the real world. Concrete and glass. Iron and steel. Hard and painful things. Damaging things. Inescapable things.

She realized she was staggering. The other woman, Arella, had come to her side. She put arms around Chloe, steadied her, held her up. She looked at this friend of her son's and realized they had so, so much in common but could not be further apart.

She tilted her head up to look into Arella's eyes. She'd bent over, without realizing it. Her stomach lurched inside her. She could escape all of this. Music. A pounding rhythm that drowned out the idea of voices.

But there were no voices, were there?

There was only Stephen. Her son. Rick's son. The demon.

He'd told the little gargoyle, Talk to me, or there will be nothing left of you but crumbs. The thing had tried to kill him. Kill her. It worked for the priest who had tried to use her as some sort of sacrifice. Chloe felt her muscles loosen. Her vision was funneling. The darkness threatening to overtake her was complete and unrelenting. If she passed out, that would be a different kind of escape. She would lose herself as effectively as she did when she was dancing.

But she fought it.

The gargoyle tried to resist. It struggled to escape, but Stephen's demonic fist was stronger. He brought the thing closer to his face so he could lower his voice. A kind of softness Rick would never have displayed. "Can you talk?"

It made a sound, something more akin to wailing stone than speech. The cry was high-pitched, unwavering, and went on for almost a full minute before it ceased its struggles.

Chloe managed to straighten herself, but Arella still held her up.

Stephen said, "Did you come after us alone?"

The thing looked straight into Stephen's eyes. It was one-third his height, but half his breadth. It had been damaged before following them here. Its stone had been scraped and chipped. Its face resembled Chloe's most severe nightmares. Things weren't where they were supposed to be, weren't quite the right size or shape. It had been chiseled roughly, not by a master, and its expression suggested pain.

Everything about the thing's existence was pain.

That's what the expression suggested, but Chloe didn't believe it. It didn't move or act like a creature in pain. Or it had learned to live with it. She pushed forward, shrugging free of Arella's support, and said, "Who are you?"

The gargoyle turned toward her. Stephen held it tight. It tried to burst free of his grip, but it didn't have the strength. It snarled instead, a soundless expression of rage that brought Chloe back to the present.

Sure, Stephen reminded her of Rick. He looked like his father. He shared his father's demon blood and maybe his temper. But he was much more reserved, whereas the little stone man with terrors banged into its face did everything it could to release all its anger.

The thing opened its mouth again, another ear-piercing sound, and twisted in Stephen's hands like an enraged cat, all its limbs, if they could be called arms and legs, and its broken wings crunching down on Stephen's hand even as it propelled itself forward.

Stephen rocked backwards. He released his hand in a spray of blood. For a moment, it seemed the gargoyle intended to pulverize Stephen's forearm, but it pushed suddenly to one side.

It went neither straight back nor up, so Stephen swiped at it but missed. The thing barreled into Chloe, and Arella immediately behind her.

Chloe cried out. Dropped back. No, she dropped down, first bouncing off Arella. She lost her breath. The speakeasy, already little more than a shroud of darkness, went utterly black.

It didn't last long. She felt herself bounce once on the tiled floor. It hurt. Pain crisscrossed her body in competing waves. She groaned, rolled clutching her chest as though something might burst from her skin. She opened her eyes, but she didn't see the gargoyle anymore. She didn't see Arella or her son. She saw nothing, a nothing that came to consume her.

<hr />

The gargoyle bounced off him and smashed into Arella and his mother. It seemed to be out of control, seeking any exit rather than to attack, but it threw Stephen's mother to the floor. Arella managed to catch herself on a table and not fall, but his mom had taken the brunt of the stone's ricochet.

Clearly, it wasn't capable of speech. But it was capable of doing tremendous damage, especially to the purely human flesh of Arella and his mother.

With his unhurt hand, Stephen pounded the side of the statue as it crashed into the ceiling. He held back nothing. He flung the majority of the statue into the nearest wall. Chunks of stone burst away like shrapnel.

He didn't wait to see if the thing could recover from the blow. He rushed after it and smashed its head into a thousand pieces.

The thing collapsed. All the pieces, whether they'd been flying or not, rained onto the floor.

Stephen, painfully but without thought, shifted back to his human form as he came to his mother's side. He knelt there, amidst the rubble that had been one of the gargoyles, and for a moment didn't know what to do.

His mother opened her eyes. Looked up at him. Smiled, albeit weakly.

Arella knelt opposite her. She checked Chloe's pulse in her throat. She said, "You still with us?"

"Stop," Chloe said, trying to push Arella's hand away.

"You're breathing," Arella said. It wasn't a question.

Chloe tried to sit up, but thought better of it. She looked from Arella to Stephen. She kept her voice at a low volume and even tempo. "What are you even doing here?"

"What?"

"Those things," Chloe said. "They've come for you, haven't they? They wanted me to draw you to them. And now they're not going to stop until they destroy you."

Stephen shook his head. "No," he said. "No, they didn't expect me."

"No one expected you," Arella said.

Stephen ignored it. He took his mother's hand. His hurt, the hand the gargoyle had tried to destroy, and it hurt more when Chloe squeezed.

After a moment's silence, which was suddenly rather thick, Arella asked, "Is anything broken?"

"No," Chloe said.

"Where does it hurt?"

Chloe shook her head. "Everything hurts. Are you a nurse?"

"I'm an artist."

"Oh, that's great," Chloe said. When Arella didn't respond, she added, "He cut me. Not the statue, the priest."

"I don't think he was a priest," Stephen said.

"Whatever he was, he cut me, and I bled, and I—I don't know, I feel it, inside me and out, the blood doing whatever it was he intended to do."

"What do you mean?" Stephen asked.

"He didn't need me to die," Chloe said. "He wanted

that. I think that's obvious, isn't it? But he only needed my blood."

"So whatever ceremony he was performing," Arella said, "he performed."

"I think so."

"How do you know this?" Stephen asked.

Chloe shook her head and, slowly, sat up. "I've felt a lot of things in my life, Stephen. Heartbreak. Fear. Futility. And I've tried desperately not to feel anything at all. It never works, did you know that? The feelings always come back." She took a breath. "I feel my blood, Stephen. In a way I don't think I'm supposed to. I feel it flowing through my veins, I feel it oozing down my chest, and I feel it on the edge of that black blade. It's still there. He won't ever clean it off. I think I can feel every drop of my blood. A trail of it leading back to St. Lazarus'. And some of it, I felt, before it became something else. Before it..." She paused to find a word. "Before it became part of the air. Before it became part of something else. I can't feel those drops anymore, Stephen, but when I felt them last, they felt like stone."

CHAPTER 23

Pierce whispered a command. No one heard him. Despite the millions of people living in the city, despite the hundreds he could probably count at this moment at or near the site of the cathedral, where the crowd had been building and dispersing at about equal measure, his command was not for human ears.

He said, "Amass."

He might've said, A mass, but he paid careful attention to his articulation. And even if it had been misheard, the result would still be the same.

He added, "Midnight."

Around him, near and far, the statues of New York City stirred. Some tilted their heads to better hear and understand. Some vacated their plinths. Others took to the skies, to the streets, to the tunnels underground.

Those that were nearest understood the unspoken aspects of the command. They retreated from the world. Slipped into the deepest shadows and crevices. Took to the alleys and rooftops. Disappeared from view.

The continued police presence at the cathedral was only a minor problem. They wouldn't be there long. It wasn't an active crime scene. Merely a place where someone had dropped some meat.

The fact that the meat had been a human heart, they might not even know yet.

He wasn't sure how they were handling it. But he knew, from the priest, that it had briefly become the only thing New Yorkers wanted to talk about. Already, however, the rest of the city had moved on. There were schedules to keep. No minor mystery would distract them for long.

In another hour, this wouldn't be any bigger than a rat running up from the subway with a slice of pizza.

That reminded him. He should eat.

His statues—his army—had no need for food. Or rest. Soon, they would have no need of anything.

He did not return to his apartment. It was a small, meager thing, up near the top of the city, filled with books and candles, jars of feathers, swaths of fabrics, notepads and fountain pens, all his observations and lessons learned. What he really needed, however, was The Book of Lost Fates, which that woman had snatched.

She couldn't be just some normal thief. She'd arrived with the demon, or at least at the same time. He didn't believe in coincidence. The three of them, both women and that infernal beast, were lined up against him. He couldn't afford to think otherwise.

First, there was the matter of his friend. The priest. The man who had set him upon this particular journey so many years ago. Merely a priest then, not a bishop, not a cardinal, not anyone of any great importance. A man, made of flesh, blood, and bone. A man who knew all his secrets. A confessor, a confidante, and a teacher.

A liability.

The priest was coming. There was no getting around that. Pierce stopped at a random pizza joint to consider what to do about the thief. The demon had decimated his army, but maybe half of them were still out there, and at least a couple would've gone after the thief, the woman, and the demon. They would come back to report tonight. At midnight.

Maybe the priest would arrive around the same time.

He could give Father Constantine a good demonstration of his army's strength.

Pizza was fine. He ate mindlessly and watched the street through the window. The rain had gotten worse. That alone would drive some of the crowd away. The fence would be restored. Maybe even his friend, the priest, would take care of that. He'd already be working on that. He didn't want witnesses for what he must have thought of as his great triumph.

The sun had set, but Pierce needed a place to wait before going back to the cathedral. He still remembered that long ago night in all its details. The demon—the second one, the massive creature that dwarfed even the one he'd seen tonight—had crashed through the rose window to bring death and destruction to the gargoyle.

He didn't know what had happened prior to that night. He knew about the littler demon, which the gargoyle had killed first. He didn't really know anything then about the priest or the artist—Father O'Leary and Nene Spirito—not until later. That night, he only knew the urgency in that battle. Fueled by love, by vengeance, by a sense of righteousness—all of this on both sides. He pieced a lot of it together after.

In the end, it was the artist who delivered the killing blow to the demon. She'd had a knife. A simple, ceremonial blade, probably not much different than the one he carried now.

The gargoyle didn't survive it, either.

Years later, perhaps by God's wrath, St. Lazarus' Cathedral was ripped out of the heart of New York City.

He hadn't known then the story behind either

demon or gargoyle. He didn't really care. He'd stayed hidden. He'd come in only for shelter. For respite. He hadn't expected to see the culmination of anything.

And now, he was on the verge of his own culmination.

The demon had come to stop him, but this time there was only one — he assumed it was the last of them, a line of them, something passed down from father to son. He'd witnessed two generations of demon destroyed. This would be the last of them.

He never knew who had given breath to that gargoyle.

But this time, he had more than a single gargoyle. The statues of New York were all behind him now. Maybe even the big ones. Atlas, outside Rockefeller Center. The Wall Street bull. The brave girl, whatever they called her. Pierce already knew it wasn't just stone that answered his call. Marble. Bronze. Iron. Steel. They were out there, in all forms and all sizes, ready to listen to his every command.

From the pizza shop, he saw them. Architectural flourishes on dozens if not hundreds of buildings. Artwork in fancy galleries. Museums. He should have performed the spell work nearer to The Met. They had ancient statues from India, China, and Egypt, including pharaohs and gods!

He could have commanded the statues from the Wax Museum at Times Square.

He wondered how many adjustments his spell would require to give him the Statue of Liberty. Or the Sphinx. China's army of terracotta warriors! What better way to build an army than to add an already existing army?

Pierce took a breath, and another bite of pizza, and tried to calm down. He was getting way too far ahead of himself. First, he needed to test the limits of his control, as well as the limits of what his army would do for him.

He would start with his friend, the priest. And the demon, who had come to stop him.

He would start, and it would be glorious.

⸙

She watched the window from the rooftop. She had severed the threads that bound her and the infant gargoyle to him, but no one else could give her what she truly wanted.

Breath.

Real, honest breath, into lungs that worked like any other lungs.

Her previous life had been cruel and short. This stony existence had stretched far too long already. She could move, but certainly he had been intending to do more than give her—and the others—movement.

The rain washed clean the blood of her sins. When she returned to a life of flesh, she could worry about the things she might feel, emotions like regret and anger and sorrow. For now, she recognized only the distant echo of these things. Like her fingers, her heart was stone and therefore felt nothing.

Nothing but a fleeting inkling of hope.

He had done more. He had brought forth others. They were stone, too, or other materials, but none of them lived. None of them breathed. None of them had hearts pumping blood through their veins. Like her, they had no veins.

She saw them, though. They were everywhere now.

A dozen or a hundred. She didn't bother to count. They meant nothing to her or her infant. The thread connecting her to the gargoyle had gotten stronger, even when it had gone underground in search of the book of magic that would grant her and her baby another chance.

CHAPTER 24

In the middle of the speakeasy, Chloe sat cross-legged and rocked back and forth. She tried not to look at anyone anymore. The gargoyles were too much. Her son—Rick's son—was too much. She couldn't count the ways in which she'd failed him. Over and over again. Even his conception was a failure of some sort, though she didn't know then what Rick was or what their son would become.

She stole glances at him now and then, through the darkness shrouding the speakeasy, and she'd led them to this place which couldn't possibly protect them. How many holes in the floors, walls, and ceilings would lead their enemies directly to them?

The shattered pieces of one gargoyle were more than sufficient evidence. Others knew where they were. Others would come.

She hugged her legs to her chest and let her knees support her head.

Her son and his friend were talking, but she couldn't focus on the words anymore. She knew she'd been doing good. Real good. For a moment, she'd had clarity, she'd had cohesion, she'd had some grasp on at least a semblance of reality, but it was slipping away again and she knew she would never really catch it. Reality wasn't a thing that could be caught. It was slippery. Oiled up. A wriggling, writhing, contemptuous thing that absolutely did not want to be captured.

She could have her music. Her dancing. Her sex.

That brought her back to Stephen. He was a result of that. Music, dancing, sex with demons. She hadn't been thinking then, and thinking now came no more easily.

Time for thinking was done. Time for memories was past. All that remained was to act. To move. To take the battle to their enemies.

She said, "We have to go."

She wasn't sure she'd said it aloud. She might've just thought it. She curled deeper into herself. Everything scared her. Everything scarred her. She wasn't going to get out of this life alive.

She said, "We have to stop him."

She lifted her head off her arms, off her knees, a real and honest attempt to escape the ball of crap she was retreating into. She took a breath, a deep one, meant to banish all of everything fermenting inside her.

Stephen knelt in front of her. Looked straight at her with Rick's eyes.

No. Not Rick's. Rick was dead. The gargoyle had killed him twenty years ago. Two decades. Half her life ago. So much had happened since then, so much that she hadn't seen, hadn't registered, had in fact ignored.

Stephen looked at her with his own eyes. She saw fear there, multiple layers of it. He still didn't know what was happening to him. He had no idea what he'd gotten involved with here. She saw hope, too, and kindness, a gentleness which his demon of a father had been incapable. She saw wonder, too, and curiosity, an array of emotions and characteristics she couldn't possible see in a split second.

But when she focused, when she tried, when she put effort into it, her perceptions were extraordinary. That's why she had to escape them so often. What she saw, what she felt — it could all be so overwhelming. She had no choice but to shut down. She had no choice but to run away.

Not today.

Her son—hers, not his—needed her help.

She said, "Or he won't stop."

"Who is he?" Stephen asked.

Chloe shook her head. Harder than she'd intended. She shook off drops of rainwater. Her voice barely escaped her. "I have no idea."

His friend, the woman, Arella—her age, not Stephen's age—was beside her, had an arm wrapped around her shoulders. How long had she been there? This whole time? Arella asked, "How many of those statues does he have?"

"Gargoyles," Chloe said. "They're all gargoyles, just like the first time."

No one asked her about the first time. Maybe they knew.

"Maybe they're not gargoyles," Chloe said, "but they are. Absolutely. They're meant to protect the church, right?"

"Not exactly," Arella said.

Chloe shook her head again. She wouldn't listen to arguments now. She was in the middle of something. "He is their church. Last time, it was a woman, an artist." She spoke so fast, the words spilled from her and ran over top each other. "He protected her, saved her, redeemed her, and...and...maybe it was some kind of magic that made him then, just like it was some sort of magic now." Her eyes went wide. Wild. She felt them grow in her face. "Maybe he did it then, too, but I don't think so, Stephen. I don't think it was him. It must've been his father. His Father, you know. The priest at

St. Lazarus' Cathedral when it all happened. Father O'Leary."

"I know about him," Stephen said. "He disappeared years ago. There's no one attached to what happened at the cathedral anymore."

"There's me," Chloe said. "And no one knows about me."

"Maybe he does," Arella suggested.

Chloe looked at her. She was beautiful but ragged. In that moment, Chloe saw what her son saw, and it made her smile. "Then he learned about me," Chloe said, "from his father."

Silence followed.

Silence was dangerous. Chloe had run out of words. But the weight of silence threatened to stop them before they started. She didn't really know what to do, but she knew where it had to be done. "We're connected," she said, her pace slower now as she sought words and phrases and thoughts, as she struggled to maintain them. "By St. Lazarus' Cathedral."

"A church that doesn't even exist," Stephen said.

"It does," Arella said. "The grounds exist. Its memory. Its history. And you're not the only person left who was connected."

Chloe didn't understand, but she couldn't find words to voice it.

Stephen did. He said, "The artist. Neve Spirito."

<hr />

With one hand, not letting go of Chloe because the woman needed something to bind her to reality and somehow she'd become a part of that, Arella fished out her phone. Battery was low. Of course. They'd been gone a long while. But no signal reached them in this speakeasy. It was like they hadn't just escaped through the forgotten architecture of New York City's past, but into that past. No messages were visible, no calls were getting through. There was nothing to connect them to the world.

"Your mother's right," Arella said. "We can't stay here." She looked at the remnants of the gargoyle that had chased after them. "There's more of them. A lot more."

"Beyond count," Chloe said in a whisper.

Arella shook her head. "We have to assume he didn't complete what he was doing, not the way he wanted to. He might have more of these gargoyles, but he doesn't have all of them. He doesn't have an army." She frowned. "Not more of an army than he'd already had."

"What does he want?" Stephen asked.

"What does it matter?" Chloe asked.

Stephen couldn't answer that. Neither could Arella. She said, instead, "Let's lean on the side of hope, shall we? We came to the cathedral tonight, this night, and found you." She looked directly at Chloe when she said it. The woman smiled weakly.

"But I never left," Chloe said. "I'm stuck there."

Arella nodded. "We were there tonight for a reason. We interrupted him, didn't we? Disrupted his ceremonies. Stole his shadow book." She held it up. The others stared at it as though they had never known it existed. "So he can't do it again, right? Not properly. Not without making a mistake. Right now, we have to believe he's weak because of it. But he's looking for it. He wants this. If for no other reason, he's going to keep coming for this."

Stephen asked, "What do you propose?"

"First," Arella said, "we burn the book."

Chloe pulled suddenly away from her.

"That way, even if we fail, he can't do it again."

"No," Chloe said, quickly and easily snatching the book from Arella's hands. "If we're going to undo what he's done, this is the only way."

Stephen, kneeling in front of his mother for this whole conversation, stood up. "Stay here," he said. "Keep the book safe. I'll go back."

"No," Arella said.

"He has to," Chloe said, wiping a tear from her eyes.

"There's no choice," Stephen said, directly to Arella. "Because this isn't just the night we came to the cathedral, and it isn't just the night we found my mom. It's also the day I transformed."

And he did so, in front of her. His muscles rippled under his skin. Bones cracked audibly. His body unstitched itself and put together another shape, that of the demon, so quickly most people wouldn't see the pain of it in Stephen's eyes. Those did not change, did they? Not fundamentally, no. They still belonged to him.

The demon took a deep breath. Let it out slowly. Every time he switched, the transformation repaired the broken parts of his body, the rips and tears, the cuts, no matter how deep.

The demon shifted back into Stephen's shape.

He smiled at her. For her. It felt sincere, but it didn't reach deep into him. He didn't say anything more. He went to the door, and through the door, and returned to the dark labyrinth beneath New York.

CHAPTER 25

Stephen moved with a sense of confidence he had never really lacked, but with increased intensity. All his senses sharpened in the dark, even his vision. He saw through the murk and shadows. He saw the spiders and the rats and the eyes of the lost staring at him, seeing something not entirely human—though he would've passed.

He was something else now.

The demon pulsed through his veins. It made him stronger. Did it make him smarter? It certainly made him more dangerous. He'd always struggled to keep his temper controlled, especially after the stories his grandfather told him.

Stories about his father. His father, dead before he was born.

This was his legacy. Stephen's fists curled of their own accord in response to just the thought.

There was no one to blame. His mother had run away, but maybe that had been the sanest thing to do. She was a broken woman. An ineffective mother. But smart enough to know she couldn't take care of a child. She'd given him up to her own father.

But he didn't really know the things Stephen needed to know. No one did. So now, he learned through experience. The demon surged through his veins, through his muscles, and tingled in the marrow at the center of his bones. He heard the twitches of cockroaches. Heartbeats, even through walls of concrete and brick and steel. The echoing of footsteps, thousands of them, on the city sidewalks above him.

He heard distant sirens, cries of agony and despair,

arguments, confessions of love, everything. Most of it fell away to the sides. Most of it didn't interfere. He was focused on protection, self-preservation, the defeat of an enemy he didn't know who had taken his mother's blood to create more of those statues.

Those gargoyles.

He couldn't live with that. They would hound him. They would stalk his mother until they destroyed her. They would find and terrify and torture Arella just because she'd dared to help him.

The man, the priest, whatever he was—he was out there. His gargoyles had failed to hold him down. Stephen had destroyed a few of them, pulverized them with repeated blows of immeasurable strength, rendering them into nothing but rubble.

But they had numbers enough to chase him.

Arella could work through the book. She could find a way to undo the magic that had created the statues. He would give her that time. He would take the battle to the stone and, if possible, the flesh.

Before he found the man, though, he knew his gargoyles would flock to protect him.

A ripple of the change went through him. He felt it prickling under his skin, stroking his muscles from the inside. He could get used to the pain. But not to the constant threat.

He went back the way they'd come. He didn't think it would be so easy a trail to follow, but maybe the demon also improved his sense of direction.

He had to stop thinking of it as a demon. It was inside him. A part of him. Not something or someone different. It didn't possess him. It was something he unleashed. But he was in control. Except when his temper took over. His anger. His fury. But he was no comic book rage monster, no Hyde and Jekyll.

He fully intended to let loose the monster when he found another of the gargoyles. And he would utterly destroy the man to stop him from doing all of this again.

Because it should've been a simple day. It should've been him dealing with this transformation. He had Arella's support. He had his mother. He had the hole that had been St. Lazarus' Cathedral. Maybe he also needed the gargoyle. His father had challenged one and lost. His grandfather, on the demon's side, had fallen to that same gargoyle. But it had been stronger and bigger, as far as he could tell, and fully sentient. These little things the priest enslaved were mindless automatons incapable of—what had Arella said?—redemption.

When the tunnels opened up, when he had distance to the sides and even above him, when subway cars rumbled past switches in the tracks, he smelled the hollow rancid odors of bodies wasted by drugs but not yet dead. He saw animals, not just the rats he expected, not just the insects—dogs, possums, a goose, maybe a coyote. He wasn't a zoologist. He didn't know a thing by its vague outline. Bats. He should've expected those. But he also saw unnatural things.

Men who weren't men slipping deeper into shadows. A phantom lingering invisibly on platform. Sentinels guarding doors or passageways, unmoving except for their eyes, who maybe regarded him as one of their own. He even saw statues. Unmoving. Uncaring. Things that saw him but had been sculpted for other purposes.

The city was rich with these mysteries. Bloated with them.

So the man didn't control all the statues. He was playing at whatever he thought he was doing. His

ARMY OF BLOOD AND STONE

imaginings far outweighed his actual skills. The awareness, if not knowledge, of other things in the dark gave Stephen a sense of inevitability. The man controlling these statues had not stirred any of the other things prowling through the shadows of the city into action. Therefore, he could not really be a problem. Or a threat. Stephen's mission, whatever drove him now to find the man, would succeed.

Because the things in the dark would've moved to protect themselves and their own interests. Wouldn't they?

He had to undo the man's work, and undo the man—he didn't think of it as murder, but as something wholly justified—and the dark around him would give him room enough to succeed or fail on his own.

So maybe he wasn't fighting for the city and the world. Maybe it was only for him and his mother and Arella.

That was enough.

Father Constantine rode in the back of a long black car with tinted windows and a chauffeur whose name he didn't know. James, perhaps, or William, or maybe Michael.

His bulk took half the seat. He had a wrestler's body. He had wrestled in high school and, briefly, in a semi-professional circuit, before turning his attention to his devotion. He hadn't been undefeated, but he'd won more often than not. He'd also boxed, but that was something of a cliché for men of the cloth, wasn't it?

He didn't like to think of himself as a cliché.

Indeed, he didn't like to think of himself as a priest,

either, despite the title. He had arranged for his position through careful manipulations, innuendoes, and when necessary, outright threats. He knew more books than just the ones revered by the church. He had read books by magicians considered anathema to the church, codices involving the natural and unnatural world, the Daemonolateria, various confessions, books of laws and lies. He had studied in Cairo, Shanghai, Cité Soleil, academies across the globe. His position gave him some sovereignty over the site of St. Lazarus' Cathedral. The nature of that building, or more precisely, the lack of that building, allowed him a degree of autonomy.

Through the window, he watched the rain. It didn't merely fall, but it didn't wash clean the city of its sins. It echoed cracks in the filaments of existence. The rain nailed the sky to the earth, at least to this city, because otherwise, it might all come undone.

That was the kind of work Pierce had accomplished.

He nearly allowed himself to smile.

Pierce had been a wild card. Constantine never expected him to succeed at anything, though he could still be used here and there for certain jobs that required discretion. His mind was broken by the things he'd witnessed, which made him easily malleable but also unpredictable and unreliable.

Until, of course, he had managed to accomplish something.

The car pulled off the street and descended to a private, underground garage. Small, containing only five spots, it was empty. It did not belong to the church. Neither did this car or its driver.

He was not a priest who gave mass. Technically, he had ascended beyond the titles of Priest. It worked in his favor to maintain that illusion under most circumstances. He traveled the world doing the good work, especially when that good work benefited him directly.

He was here to do that good work now.

The driver opened his door. He climbed out. He detested the smell of this city, of most cities. He didn't like having people so closely crowded together. He preferred a more intimate setting for most things.

He said nothing to the driver. He walked to the elevator like a kind of a god. It brought him up to the ground level. He emerged in a hall that included other elevators that rose into the building they'd parked beneath, but the residents who lived above would never use his elevator. It didn't go where they wanted to go.

The hall took him to the streets of New York City He turned to his right and saw the spot where St. Lazarus' Cathedral had once proudly stood. He'd been here, once or twice, back before the building disappeared. It had been brought low by wicked magic, but not his. It had descended to a kind of hell of persistent night. He'd come after the first incident— with the gargoyle. He had interrogated Father O'Leary directly and had learned much.

That priest had gone off in search of the cathedral after their next conversation, when it seemed that nothing remained of the cathedral. That wasn't entirely true. Constantine had spent several days overseeing the removal of potentially important pieces. He hadn't expected much of anything to ever matter from here.

It was, as far as he'd been concerned, a dead site. Dead to the world, dead to the church, and dead to him.

But Pierce had always been something of a dreamer. He followed a voice in his head, a path he hadn't forged, a plan he could never have derived on his own. Constantine had allowed it, had even encouraged it, because the man had proven somewhat useful.

Through the rain, he approached the fence. One gate, boarded up and fairly well obscured, opened onto the site. There were other ways in, through the underground, but Constantine didn't need that kind of subtlety at the moment. His key allowed him entrance. He saw where the police had been, where Pierce had done his work. They had gathered their evidence, presumably, and searched the ruins of the cathedral, but abandoned it to yellow tape. The fence, where it had been damaged, had been boarded up already.

Constantine had seen to that.

He locked the gate behind him. He admired the rough, sketchy nature of the altar and its arrangement of pews. Pierce had always been somewhat grandiose in his ideas, but had he actually tried to claim himself as the priest here?

Constantine looked to the sky, to the skyline around the site. He saw the gaps. The absences. The empty spots.

He took a deep breath. He reached through the rain, took hold of unseen threads, and tightened the net around the site. St. Lazarus' Cathedral belonged to him. He would have it and all that it contained. He would decide how best to utilize what came from it.

And he and Pierce would have a long overdue conversation.

ARMY OF BLOOD AND STONE

CHAPTER 26

Pierce watched Constantine enter the site of St. Lazarus' Cathedral. No, he did more than watch. He felt the man's arrival. Through the threads that connected him to the place, through the spell work he'd performed, through the blood flowing through the veins under stone skin.

His gargoyles saw the man arrive. Man, priest, bishop, Father—whatever he called himself, whatever he was, he drew on the site and from the site in a way Pierce couldn't comprehend. The man stepped onto that land, that landfill, that empty space where once upon a time a gargoyle and demon fought till they'd both died.

Constantine owned the space. He controlled the air it breathed and the power inherit within. Pierce saw this now, in ways he never could before, more thoroughly and deeply, and he saw it through the eyes of one of his gargoyles.

She had given him one of the eyes. She'd protected both. The essence of her, stone dust and all, had gotten inside those orbs. She'd given it to him without a word, the hazel one, then pointed to her own eye.

Her meaning was clear.

Then she'd left him.

He looked now at the eye, the swirling colors inside, a bit of fading green, gold and brown, lifeless and sightless but still somehow meaningful. In that iris, underneath the colors, an image formed.

Pierce had watched Constantine from down the street. Through the eye, he saw what the statue saw: Constantine from above. On the inside. Sketching sigils in the air. Soundlessly casting his own layer of spells.

Pierce's heart quickened. His anger grew. Constantine had been using him. Guiding Pierce to his own nefarious purposes.

"My purposes now," Pierce whispered, but the words felt limp as soon as they entered the air. The rain hammered them down, cracked them upon the sidewalk, shattered them into their worthless component parts. Pierce narrowed his eyes. He had trained for this, or been trained for this, and it was time to pay his respects.

He raised his head. Welcomed the wash of rain upon his head, streaming down his cheeks and back. In a way, the rain was the blood of the city. It nourished him. Fortified him for what was ahead.

He strode down the street. He didn't ignore everything around him, but he disregarded most of it. Yes, there were the statues, little pieces of the world that had answered his call. Some admired him. Rejoiced in him. Followed him and would fight for him. Others went ahead, responding to the nearly irresistible pull of Constantine.

In another time, he might not have to do this. But some gravities were inescapable.

He noticed police and other authorities. He saw EMTs drenched in the rain. People, the meaningless kind, gathering in mobs. None of them noticed him. He looked like one of the meaningless kind. For a long time, he wore it. As a disguise. As though it was something to be proud of. He didn't bother with a thought for them now. He focused on the only thing he could.

He approached the former site of the cathedral.

Every drop of rain felt like a pinprick of ice. Every heartbeat hammered with impossible heat. He felt stone dust in his veins, not just blood. He wasn't becoming one of them. They weren't becoming extensions of him.

He looked down only to glance at the image in the eye. It showed Constantine turning in his direction. Smiling. He was close now, and the statue had moved closer. The rest of the world faded away at the edges.

Pierce had to descend to the subways. He understood the symbology of this, though he doubted it applied. He moved through that labyrinth like a mouse following a scent. He touched the tiled walls, the rusted support beams that held up the surface.

When he ascended, he felt a little like a god. He heard the gargoyles beside him and behind him.

He rose into rain. Into the empty space of St. Lazarus' Cathedral. He recognized the spires in their absence. Felt the echoes of moonlight falling through a rose window shattered some two decades previous. He met the eyes of Constantine.

He was a huge man. He towered over Pierce even when they stood upon level ground, but somehow the sloped earth beneath them lifted Constantine even higher so that he looked down at Pierce. Derisively. Disappointedly. Angrily.

The man's voice betrayed none of that when he spoke. "You have done well," Constantine said with some trace of a smile. "Now give them to me."

Looking into Constantine's eyes felt like looking into twin abysses. They threatened to swallow and pulverize Pierce. They made his knees weak. He looked away, downward, and saw something in the eye he hadn't expected to see.

The statue had come closer.

He looked up. He shouldn't have. He gave away the gargoyle's presence too soon. She had gotten closer, but not close enough. Constantine turned, his head and the upper bulk of him, to see her approaching. She had no wings, but had been hopping gingerly to lower heights until she'd reached the ground. She had been one of Pierce's first. She'd been moving to protect him from the threat.

From Constantine.

With a flick of his hand, he stopped her. The statues behind Pierce, whom he'd thought had been fully in support of him, surged forward.

These were the new ones. They had no loyalty. No honor. They rushed forward, pushing and scraping past Pierce, a river of gargoyles in stone and plastic and resin, and swarmed the female statue who had gotten him his eyes.

They came in a variety of sizes, none much taller than Pierce's knees, some only as large as fists. Yet they overwhelmed her. They forced her to her knees.

"Yes, yes," Constantine said, stepping closer to the statue, holding out his hands. He sounded as though he approved of her and her actions. He found something in them commendable. He extended one of his hands, palm up, and said, "I believe you have something for me."

The statue never really struggled. She didn't fight. From the moment Constantine had fixed his attention on her, it seemed she'd lost her ability to move of her own accord. Instead of resisting, but with a possibly deliberate slowness that stretched the moment to impossible lengths, she lifted one of her arms.

Not the attacking arm. Not the hand she meant to raise against Constantine. She opened her closed fist over Constantine's open hand and dropped the other eye into it.

His back was to Pierce, who also seemed to have lost his ability to move, but still it seemed the man had smiled broadly at this gesture.

Constantine turned toward Pierce. He said, "You learned well from me, Pierce. You asked for things of power. A heart, I see the remnants of, and eyes. These two." He held up the blue eye. The hazel burned in Pierce's hand. "But the power in this one is already fading. After death, the eyes are quick to lose their strength. No fresh blood in them."

He popped it into his mouth, made a show of chewing for a moment, then swallowed. "Still tasty, though." He held out his hand to Pierce. "The other, if you would."

Tentatively, with a quick glance at the impassive face of his best gargoyle, Pierce handed over the hazel eye. Did she wince? Did she—smile? Was she capable of either, or was Pierce projecting his own convoluted emotions?

Constantine hardly looked at this second eye. He swallowed it whole, then licked the tips of his fingers.

Lightning erupted not too distantly behind him, dancing amongst the Manhattan skyline. The roar of thunder came instantaneously.

"Now," Constantine said, an army of statues growing around him and staring painfully into Pierce's heart and soul, "I believe it's time I collect what you owe me."

CHAPTER 27

Stephen rose from the subways, from the maze beneath the city, into darkness and noise and relentless rain. Thunder roiled in the distance and clamored close. He felt the lightning even when he didn't see it. The pulse of the city throbbed all around him.

He was not the center of the storm.

That would be St. Lazarus'. Where the man commanded gargoyles.

Here, he saw them, the big and the small, in numbers beyond count. They made their way mindlessly through the city toward the cathedral. They answered a call Stephen did not hear. When he looked directly at one, it noticed him but then continued on its way.

It hadn't received the instruction to destroy him.

The priest had grown his army.

They looked back at him lifelessly and thoughtlessly. They followed a single directive. Stephen moved in the same direction. He didn't know what would happen when he got there. He didn't know how he could face an army of those things. So many were so small, but they were just that: so many.

The demon within him rippled beneath his skin. He restrained it now only with great effort. As he got closer to the cathedral, it became harder to hold back. He walked more quickly until he broke into a run.

Chloe kept pacing the abandoned speakeasy, muttering as she did, stopping on occasion to stare at something in the wall or in the darkness. Sometimes, she looked at Arella long enough she had to pause in her reading.

The book was fascinating, at least in the parts that she could read. It talked about demons. Cities hidden under oceans. Wizards and kings.

Not all of the illustrations were recognizable. Some were labeled. Some were partial, like the one showing one side of a man. Diagrams of leaves and flowers. Geometric symbols. Eyes like out of Egypt.

And so, so much she couldn't read. Some passages were obviously Latin, which was beyond her. More were in languages that might've been Spanish or Italian. Others were written with other alphabets, not just the Cyrillic she recognized but others she couldn't begin to decipher. Some of it might be written in codes not readily decipherable by anyone alive.

The priest had worked out quite a bit. Arella certainly hadn't gotten as far.

"Listen to this," she said, interrupting Chloe's pacing. "A spirit can become trapped within stone, often as a punishment, often self-inflicted but sometimes by someone else's design. Such statues are difficult to control, though their guilt can be used against them. However, a stone does not need to be inhabited to become animated." She looked up. "This is what he used to bring those things to life."

Chloe stared blankly back at her. Was Stephen's mother even with her anymore? What was she thinking? Was she thinking at all or merely reacting?

"Chloe," she said.

The other woman blinked and seemed to refocus on

her. Almost under her breath, she said, "Rick fought one of those. The inhabited ones."

"That's not what we're dealing with here," Arella said. "And I think we can undo it."

"Think?"

"It requires blood," Arella said with a grin. "From the same source as the blood that made them rise."

Chloe shook her head briefly, then nodded, then also grinned. "Mine."

But Arella frowned. "I can't make out all of this. So I don't know for certain."

"But we have someplace to start," Chloe said, life returning to her voice.

———

She got closer.

She didn't move clumsily. Perhaps she should have. She didn't understand the mechanics of how she moved. She had been flesh, once upon a time, living a life that hadn't mattered then and didn't matter now, dying a meaningless and painful a death she probably didn't deserve.

And now, a second chance was within her grasp.

She willed her heart to beat. It did not. It was stone. It didn't move like her fingers, like her neck, like her wings.

It remained useless and dead inside her.

But echoes of the heart that had beat within her chest reverberated inside her now. It loosened the stone dust around her joints. In turn, the rain washed dust away.

She descended to a better vantage point. She watched the man, the spell caster, the priest who had revived her and all the others.

He stood within the sanctuary of his cathedral. No, he cowered. He stood in the shadow of a giant of a man, and this other—he owned and commanded the site of the former cathedral. The energy of the place, the threads, wound through him and his veins. Those threads bound the two men together, the one looking so small now in comparison.

The one who could finish reviving her.

The only one who could.

She slipped soundlessly through the air, to a lower perch, then lower again, until she stood upon scaffolding inside the grounds. The metal bones of the structure barely supported her. The rain, the thunder and lightning, obscured her approach. She was almost close enough to hear the men breathe.

Her guts twisted at that.

Guts.

As if she had anything on the inside other than stone.

Her guts twisted because all she wanted was that breath.

Pierce backed away from Constantine. Images of the man flooded his head. Memories, some of them his, but others inserted as if in desperate warning. Constantine standing over graves. Lightning dancing around him, crimson lights casting hard shadows, ceremonial blades dripping blood.

Constantine stepped forward, hands held out to either side, mimicking a gesture Pierce had seen a hundred priests make. Let us pray.

This was no place for prayer. This was no time for it. Pierce would not be saved by prayer.

Tentatively, he asked, 'What?" He blinked. He swallowed the attempt at a question and made another. "What do I owe you?"

Constantine's teeth gleamed in the thrashing lightning. "An army."

They closed in from all sides. The statues Pierce had brought to life. Had given purpose to. He had made the sacrifices, woven the spell, said the words. He'd found the book, dammit, so they belonged to him.

But he'd done it all here, at the site of the missing St. Lazarus' Cathedral. Territory that belonged to a church that had bestowed control over it, over the land and the air, the bricks, the tunnels still winding through the ground beneath it, to Constantine.

The gargoyles came forth, closing in on Pierce from all sides. They peered over Constantine's shoulder. They came for Pierce, but not in answer to his call.

In answer to Constantine. Man, priest, bishop, something otherworldly. Not a man merely of the flesh.

"An army," Constantine said again, "that requires flesh blood."

Pierce took another step backwards, but his leg hit something solid, something stony, that had not been there before. One of the gargoyles that should have been his. He tried to assert control. Tried to move it by sheer strength of will. Thought at it, *Kill the other man Don't listen to him. Obey me, dammit. I brought you to life. I gave you breath.*

They didn't actually breathe, but that was arguing semantics

An answer came to him. Yes. Give me breath.

Yes, yes, anything, Pierce thought in response.

Constantine frowned. Stepped closer. Close enough now to share the air Pierce breathed. Constantine towered over him. Constantine was two or three times the man Pierce was, maybe more, an immovable brick wall by comparison.

Constantine's next words weren't for Pierce. They were a command meant for stone ears as distant church bells—not the St. Lazarus bells which had disappeared with the cathedral-sounded midnight. "Leave no trace."

CHAPTER 28

She saw the essence of that command race along the threads. She understood the intention. Felt the power of the words. The compulsion. She moved to obey, dropping to the earth immediately behind the big man. From this angle, she felt—something? Maybe nothing. It was hard to know. A stirring of something, an echo of emotion, a trick of the shadows and the lightning.

She felt fear. The man who had promised to give her breath was about to die.

She severed the threads.

Every thread connecting the big man to the land under his feet, to the statues, even to her—it was thin, hardly a thing, but those connective threads were alive. Tentacles moving, exploring, grabbing, insinuating.

She cut them all.

For a moment, the man gasped. He felt it, physically, but it wasn't enough to stop him.

It wasn't meant to be.

It was, however, enough to stop his army of blood and stone.

⌖——⌖

Pierce felt the connections break. The gargoyles all around him had been about to descend upon him, to stomp his limbs and grind his bones to dust, to bathe in his blood and sinew, to bash open his skull and smear his brains on the grounds of St. Lazarus' Cathedral.

But they stopped.

And they waited.

He felt the weight of their eyes and expectations. They wanted commands. They expected him to lead them. Pierce, not Constantine. Not the man who had guided and betrayed him.

That man had to die.

Pierce stepped forward. A thrill of energy coursed through him. He wasn't strong, not physically, but he had something more than that.

He had been here the night the first gargoyle and the demons had fought each other. He had watched, hidden in the pews of the upper level, until both were dead. The priest and the artist had left. She took her cross with her, the weapon she'd used on the demon. The weapon that had shared properties—not merely physical properties—with the sword the gargoyle had used earlier. The sword that had broken.

It had pierced the demon's chest.

Pierce had retrieved one of those pieces. It was a secret he'd kept from Constantine, one of the few, and it had made him feel powerful even on the darkest of nights.

Now, the gargoyles moved around Constantine. Grabbed his arms, his legs, to hold him in place. He struggled against them first, pulling and pushing them away, regaining himself only to be restrained again.

Then, he turned his attention on Pierce.

"This is my cathedral," Constantine told him.

Pierce gestured at the skyline around them. They were in the hole left by the absent cathedral. "Maybe it was," he said. "But I see no cathedral."

He shoved the sword shard into Constantine's chest.

It had been coated with platinum, but underneath was something more solid and more dangerous. It was a conduit for mystical energy. It hadn't served any purpose in the creation of Pierce's army. Swords were weapons. They were meant for destruction, not creation. They were meant to kill.

A twelve inch sliver of platinum and lead and steel, celestial bronze and imperial gold, slid through Constantine's flesh until it lodged into a piece of bone, perhaps a rib but perhaps his spine. It spilled its poison into the big man's body and blood. It paralyzed his nervous system, the muscles of his chest and arms and legs. He stuttered briefly, calling upon some vast power, channeling a spell, working an archaic magic.

Briefly, Pierce saw the energy gathering. But the sword had weakened Constantine. It had stolen his breath, albeit briefly. The man moved through his words slowly. He worked his fingers, forming alchemical geometries in the air.

Pierce recognized the danger.

He stepped back. He did not want to die with Constantine. The man, the priest, the bishop—whatever he was, he was short for this earth. Pierce had brought him to the end of his time. The gargoyles that held him tried to stop his fingers, yet somehow he managed to push them away.

Behind him stood the gargoyle, the realest and most powerful of them, a mother with wings and an angelic face standing as tall as any man or woman. She had cut the ties that bound the gargoyles to Constantine. Not just the gargoyles, but the whole of the site.

Her eyes focused on Pierce.

Pierce said, "Finish him."

She did not respond. She did not react at all. She heard him, he was sure of that. They had communicated without words just a moment ago, of course she heard him. But she didn't obey. She wasn't supplicant to him.

The storm answered instead.

The rain continued to fall. For a moment, the smell of ozone almost overwhelmed Pierce.

A jagged bolt of lightning dropped from the clouds. Its target: the sliver of platinum sticking out of Constantine's chest.

It spread through his veins, through his lymphatic system, lighting him up from the inside. The fist of the lightning that struck his chest was vastly larger than the tip of the sword fragment. It burned a hole through his chest and back almost half a foot in diameter.

Constantine's eyes liquefied. His fingers scorched and smoked. The words in his throat froze and broke apart, dropped with the rain, and were scattered by the winds.

Briefly, Constantine seemed to look directly at Pierce. He even lifted his arms, took a step forward, opened his charred mouth to say something.

The force of that step, the weight of it on the ground, sent a visible tremor through Constantine's body. Ash and soot fell.

None of the small gargoyles holding him had survived.

Even the tall one, the woman behind him, had been thrown backward by the force of the lightning bolt. Cracks ran through her stony flesh, edged by singe marks. As Constantine's lifeless body finally fell, Pierce stepped toward the gargoyle. He wondered why he hadn't also been hit by the spray of that lightning strike. Maybe he had been, and he hadn't felt it.

Her eyes looked up at him, but he wasn't sure he saw any sign of life. No movement. No semblance of breath. Nothing. She laid there, completely still, apparently having sacrificed herself for him.

He gave her the sign of the cross. A kind of last rites. He was no priest, never had been, but he couldn't ignore the fact that, with Constantine's destruction, St. Lazarus' Cathedral, at least the site where it had once stood, belonged spiritually to him alone.

CHAPTER 29

Stephen retreated into the shadows. The demon pulsed inside him. The rain came relentlessly and only got worse. He had just watched the man—whom he had thought of as a priest but was clearly something other—destroy an actual priest—maybe a bishop, maybe a cardinal, Stephen wasn't Catholic enough to know or care about the differences—with the help of one of his gargoyles.

The stone gargoyle was sprawled on the ground. Had she been destroyed, too? Shouldn't there be nothing left of her?

And the man, the priest, who had meant to sacrifice Stephen's mother—his poor excuse for a mother—to increase the numbers of his army. He had, in a way, succeeded. The night was alive with them. They were everywhere. In every crevice. Around every corner.

Stephen took a moment to control himself. The beast inside him was his purest, most unadulterated rage. It burned. But brute strength wasn't going to be enough to solve this. There were dozens, perhaps hundreds, maybe even thousands of gargoyles in this city that now answered to that man.

And he glowed with the power.

Whatever had been in the big priest had been real strength, and it was siphoning into his adversary. Stephen had to consider his options. If he put the man down, as he had to, would that army rise up to avenge him? Would they roam the city without commands and intention, causing who knew what level of havoc?

He might not have a choice. The gargoyles, big or small, were not a direct and active threat to his mother.

Chloe. Virtually a stranger. He couldn't give her up to him.

The man had also seen Arella. Stephen didn't know how he felt about her or what she meant to him. She understood him in a way no one ever had. No one ever could. She had knowledge and the capacity for belief. Also, she was an amazing artist and extraordinarily insightful. She, more than he, had brought them here.

He leaned forward, out of the place where he hid. The man looked directly at him. The man smiled.

"I know who you are," he said. "What you are."

Stephen stepped out of the shadows. He had clearly not hidden as well as he'd thought. All around them, the shadows shifted, the statues and gargoyles crowded closer and more tightly. They came from everywhere now. They were even behind him. No wonder he hadn't remained hidden.

"What's that?" Stephen asked. Both fists tightened of their own accord.

"I was here," the man said. "That night when the gargoyle fought the demons. I saw the whole thing. Heard everything. I was a witness, you might say. And I was scared. Then. I cowered. I hid. I stayed so completely still, I didn't even breathe until an hour after the whole thing was done. After the demons were corpses. After the gargoyle had been reduced to rubble and dust. And you." He sneered as he said it. "You must be the continuation of that line. Another demon."

The demon reverberated through him. Stephen restrained it, but only for the moment. He didn't intend to keep it inside forever. This was at an end.

"Look around," the man said. "You are hopelessly and helplessly outnumbered. I have an army of blood and stone. I have the end of you in the palm of my hand." He raised that hand, closed his fist, made it some sort of melodramatic gesture, then threw it aside and said, "You don't have to die."

Stephen felt the weight of the gargoyles around him.

"I need more blood," the man said. "And I need my book back. I will grow my army. There are —" He paused, looking for the right word. "Legions out there just waiting for me to command them."

"Why?" Stephen asked. It wasn't much of a question. He wasn't sure he cared. But the press of the gargoyles pushed him closer to the man. A little bit closer, and he could possibly strike the man down before the gargoyles stopped him. If he did nothing else before the gargoyles killed him, he could at least put an end to whatever plans this man had.

The chaos that might follow, Stephen would be unable to do anything about. That would have to fall on others.

He felt certain, now, that there were others.

His whole life, Stephen had lived with the knowledge of what was inside him. He hadn't always believed it. His grandfather had never tried to use the Bible or religion to beat it into him, but had, from before Stephen could walk, been telling him about a great evil inside him. *You can prevent it,* his grandfather had told him. *You can keep it locked away inside. You don't have to share your father's legacy. He was an evil and terrible man. He did horrible things to people. You don't have to be that. But you always have to be in control of yourself. Keep your temper tempered. Control your anger. You do not have to be what preceded you.*

But he couldn't avoid it, could he? It wasn't about his temper. He wasn't in a comic book. He had some control over it, but the demon inside wanted to create damage and destruction.

It built up inside him. Rippled just under his skin. He felt it in his bones, which were ready to break apart again and reform. He had no idea how any of it worked, how he could even survive that kind of transition. Arella had risked it. She'd taken him in—quite literally—as a man and a demon. She'd allowed him to unleash himself. He hadn't lost all control. He hadn't rampaged down Flatbush Avenue.

Arella had given him focus.

He loved her for that. He would have to tell her. Which meant, he would have to escape this. Maybe he could fly away. He had wings. He could make them work better for him now, he was sure of it. Need made it necessary. Made it possible.

His adversary had taken plenty of time to respond. Stephen had gotten closer. "Why, indeed?" the man asked. "Because it's my turn."

"Your turn?"

"All my life, I've answered to someone. My father. My teachers. My supervisor. My priest." He laughed at that. "Now, everyone and everything will answer to me. They won't have a choice. They will fear me."

No one had ever feared him. He was too thin, too scrawny, and too timid. Stephen could see it. He wasn't any sort of intellectual giant. Physically, he was as imposing as a breath. A whisper.

And he had said it with a hint of whisper. A hint, too, of malevolence. He didn't want people to answer to him. He wanted to punish anyone who did not. Under the claws, talons, teeth, and weight of his army.

The man then said, "Imagine how much they will respect me when I have a demon leading my army." The man lifted something. At first, Stephen had no idea what it was. It was small. The sliver of platinum he had stabbed the priest with. It had been scorched, and it reflected every near and distant bolt of lightning. He had pulled it out of the dead man's chest without Stephen realizing it.

It caused Stephen to stop.

Platinum. He knew it was platinum. He didn't recognize it, but he remembered something his mother had told him. In the long, long ago. Something like a fairy tale when he was barely old enough to eat cereal. Hadn't it been a platinum blade that had killed his demon father—and his father before him?

The adversary slid his finger along the edge of the blade, wetting it with—blood?

There was no way that was random.

The adversary grinned. "Can you feel it?" he asked. "Your blood. Spilt right here on these grounds. My grounds. You're nothing now but my servant, demon."

He wielded the sliver like a wand. He swung it downward. The motion echoed in Stephen's knees and dropped him to a kneeling position.

"Good, good," the adversary said, gesturing again.

The bones inside Stephen began to crackle and split. The adversary was forcing him to transform.

CHAPTER 30

Chloe tried to sit while Arella gathered the things she needed. It should be impossible to find everything here, in a long abandoned speakeasy. But Arella seemed to be finding the things easily.

"A glass bowl." A wide-rimmed glass would work. She cleaned it as best she could with the bottom of her own shirt.

"Platinum?"

That reminded Chloe of something. A sword. A knife. No, a cross, though she wasn't quite sure what made that different anymore. Something ceremonial. Something used as a blade in St. Lazarus' Cathedral that long ago night. Something else, too. Something about Rick. Her personal god and monster. She shivered at the thought, the things he'd done both good and absolutely evil, then fingered the engagement ring on her finger.

She'd never worn it. One of Rick's trophies. From the left hand of one of his forty-three victims. Or his forty-three favorite. There was no telling how many others he'd killed or merely tormented. He hadn't taken a ring from Chloe, no, of course not, he actually—the word loved almost came into her head, but she forced it back just as quickly. That had never been true. He'd never loved her. He'd owned her, body and soul.

Did he own her still, twenty years after he'd died?

He hadn't gotten a ring from the artist, either. The artist who had used that platinum cross—but he had gathered his trophies—and never got one from the woman who saw the ghost, the artist who had used it—Chloe snapped herself back to the speakeasy and said, "Platinum."

Arella looked up at her. "That's what I said."

Chloe held out her hand. Her left hand. With the engagement ring and its diamond set in platinum. "This."

Arella looked at it a moment. She seemed shocked. Had Chloe sank to that level of despair? A shiver ran through her. "No, no," Chloe said. "It was Rick's." She swallowed. "Stephen's father. The demon."

Arella's eyes went wide. "Neve told me they never found his trophy collection. His...rings, wasn't it?"

Chloe nodded, pushing her hand forward again. "Take it. Take it and use it as you need."

Arella took her hand. In the reversal of a proposal, she slipped the ring off Chloe's finger. It came free easily. It had been a little loose. It shouldn't have stuck to her so well as it had. Maybe the ring had known its new purpose.

Arella seemed completely unaware of the significance of this action, but it felt important to Chloe. Vital, even. Like something in the world had shifted around her. In a very symbolic way, not for real at all, not when she had forty-two more rings back at the house and of course Stephen, her Stephen—this was still slipping Rick's influence off of her forever. This one piece of jewelry was enough.

Arella merely went back to her list of what she needed. A glass bowl. Platinum. Stone. There was plenty of stone all around them, not just the remnants of the gargoyle Stephen had destroyed.

But Arella took a piece of that.

"I think it says herbs," Arella said. "But it's not very specific."

"No, no, of course not," Chloe said. She had stopped pacing. She understood now. "It's all symbology. It doesn't matter if you have precisely what the book says. You—we—have the intention." She went behind the bar and, with just a little bit of looking, found several small glass jars. "Mint," she said. "Basil."

"They're very old," Arella said.

"Does it say they need to be fresh?" Chloe said without waiting for an answer. "I bet it doesn't say. I bet it doesn't care. We don't have to make a cocktail. This isn't a recipe. It's a spell."

Arella seemed to consider this. Then she nodded, once and briefly, and asked, "Is there any sage?"

Chloe shook her head. "This is it. There ain't much."

Arella nodded again. Looked down at her list again.

She didn't bother to say she needed a knife. She produced one. It was a small but wicked blade. Chloe grinned. They shared that for a moment. Over the ring, the knife, their different relationships with Stephen, that was the moment they knew each other. That was the moment they became—maybe not friends, but ride or die allies.

Chloe leaned close and whispered, "Do this. Save my son. Save us all."

Arella sighed and closer her eyes. "Right. No pressure."

"You got this, girl."

That seemed to be enough. Arella went to work. She'd gathered her ingredients. Almost everything she needed. She mixed them in the way the book instructed. She said words that might or might not have been accurate. They seemed to belong to an old, old language, something old when Latin was young.

When she reached a certain point, she paused, picked up the knife, and looked at Chloe. "I need..."

It was Chloe's turn to take Arella's hand. She gave a reassuring squeeze, something she might not have been able to do last week or last night or, hell, twenty minutes ago. She took the knife from Arella and said, quietly, "I've had practice."

She cut herself.

She cut the inside of her forearm, fully aware of the scars there. Arella might not have noticed them before. Chloe followed one of those well-worn paths. She didn't dig deep. The blade felt good. Her skin opened up for it. Drops of blood welled up from her veins.

Arella guided her arm over the glass. Three, four, five drops, then Arella said, "That's enough."

And it was.

Chloe set the knife on the table and she knew, somehow, she would never need it again. She smiled. Not a grin at all.

⚓———⚓

The gargoyle whimpered. Quietly. Silently. She knew stealth was important. If they saw her, if they knew she was there, they would do to her what they'd done to that other.

The words weren't coherent in her head, but the ideas, the concepts, the intentions remained true.

She wished she had her mother with her.

She wished mother hadn't sent her on this mission. She didn't know what she was meant to do. And - and— she did feel her mother, a connection to her mother, the thread that bound them together, even if she didn't understand it. It had gotten—smaller? Weaker? She felt her mother's pain, and she felt her own, and all she wanted to do was flee into the darkness.

But—these women.

These witches.

It reminded the gargoyle of things she couldn't really see. The flames. The fire. Had it hurt? She didn't remember hurt. She didn't really remember feeling much of anything. Just her mother. Just her mother then and now.

What they were doing would be dangerous. To her, to her mother, to the bad man at the center of it all. The man who had showed her his teeth. The man who had demanded that she move, cry, scream, fly, something.

She didn't know what to do with that. She didn't know what to do at all. She'd followed them, just as mother has asked, and now she knew where they were. Mother would have to do something about it. Mother would have to stop them. She was too afraid.

She fled.

She fled, and she knew she made noise. They heard her. They shouted things. Were they also afraid? She hoped so. She hoped so very much.

She fled, upward, sensing where there might be a path to the surface. She didn't know how she knew, but she did. It was obvious and easy to find. A hole here, a shaft there, one or two vents that came to dead ends, and then to a metal circle in the ceiling above her.

She pushed through it. She was a gargoyle. It didn't require strength. It didn't require will. It required only direction. She pushed up.

And a giant screaming thing of plastic and metal and rubber slammed into her.

She barely felt it. She knew a part of her broke away. A finger maybe. A tooth. A stone feather maybe. The massive thing, faces behind glass, a startled driver—she almost understood it to be a conveyance, an automobile, a car—no, bus. She'd put a dent in it. It had put a dent in her. The manhole cover had dropped back into place as if she'd never been there.

She rose into the air.

She rose high.

She liked the height. She liked flying with her mother, but she loved doing it on her own. It was freedom, though maybe she didn't quite understand what that meant. It was fun. It was joyous. The gargoyle giggled. The gargoyle soared. The gargoyle followed an invisible thread that would lead her to her mother.

CHAPTER 31

The first transformation had been painful but, under Arella and bound to her bed, it had not been without its pleasures. This time, the pain was magnified a thousand times. And it went excruciatingly slowly. Stephen resisted at first, then tried to force it through to completion, but the priest, with his platinum sliver wetted by Stephen's blood, did everything he could to stretch it out.

Every bone inside him cracked and snapped and broke. Not in only one or two places. Each was pulverized. Crumbled to dust in a succession of individual breaks, so that Stephen felt the agony of each and screamed with each.

The priest was absolutely gleeful as he ground Stephen's bones to dust.

His muscles, his organs, the sinew and cartilage, all the things that made up his physical body, even the nails of his fingers and toes, his eyes, the vessels that carried his blood and the blood itself, came apart at a subatomic level. Cells ruptured. Molecules collapsed. Stephen's human form sloughed away in slow, oozing rivulets of indefinable goo.

Simultaneously, the demon's body coalesced inside him. This wasn't merely a ripple that tickled under his skin. This was a complete terraforming of his physical being. The demon's organs came together with the detritus of his human form, bound by sulfur and brimstone and other fiery things. Parts weren't directly adapted. Blood didn't become the magma in his demonic veins. Those weren't made up of human veins. Nothing of the human remained whole.

Somewhere distant, very distant, Stephen heard the priest's maniacal laughing. There might even have been words, though none made it through to him. Human ears were gone. He heard entirely differently He listened at another wavelength. He didn't become something more than human, stronger to the point of superhuman, but became something other.

Acids formed inside the flesh that made up his demonic stomach.

It wasn't mere anger that fueled this transformation. It was fury. Abhorrence. Not just pain, not just heat, not just a rendering and re-structuring of flesh.

New bones formed of iron instead of calcium.

Sharp teeth. Claws that might've been talons. A sandpaper tongue. A pit of liquid fire in his entrails that scorched him from the inside.

His newly forming body borrowed from the environment around him, the dirt and stone on the ground, the air itself, to remix and remake atoms of oxygen and nitrogen into iron.

The pain began to subside. It would never go fully away. The demon's form was meant to be one of constant torment and unrelenting terror even from the inside. On the outside, he was bigger than he'd ever been, stronger by far, muscles bulging as they formed, clothes tearing. The driving rain never touched him, dissipating into steam from the heat emanating from his body. In many ways, he was a walking furnace, one filled with rage and chaos.

The emotions overrode everything else inside him.

He forgot his name. He forgot he'd had a name. He focused his attention on the priest, the man with the wand, the platinum and blood by which he was being controlled. That blood belonged to an entirely different version of him. He had transformed on every level, from his heart to his soul. He growled. He lowered his head. There were horns there now, sharp and jagged things meant to gouge and shred.

The priest backed away. He swung his little platinum wand like its magic would have some sort of an effect on the demon now.

The demon reached out, catching the hand at the wrist and crushing it. He snatched the little weapon. Examined it. Turned it over in his hands even as his body was completing its metamorphosis.

As far as he was concerned, it was fuel.

He thrust it into his body.

It barely pierced his skin. He shoved it in until it disappeared, so that the very structure of it would break down and contribute to his becoming. So that it could never again be used against him.

The priest pulled a piece of stone off a chain around his neck. A fragment from the gargoyle that was. The gargoyle that had died here fighting the demons before him. He swiped it away like it didn't matter, because it didn't.

The priest took another step back. His face contorted into something between impotent anger and abject terror. He said things, more words, more commands, but the demon would hear none of it and understood less.

The stone creatures all around him, however, did.

The gargoyles turned en masse on him.

They lunged. They hammered at him with their stone fists, drove edged weapons of wings and hands into his skin, tried to pummel and skewer him.

When the demon caught a gargoyle, he crushed it. When he swung a fist, he shattered stone into a thousand pieces. He grabbed one and flung it into another. He pulped their stony bodies, leaving behind dust and the barest fleeting memories. He grabbed two and ground them into each other.

With every gargoyle he annihilated, he drove another step closer to the priest.

He didn't think. He didn't reason. He didn't even know the true source of the anguish that coursed through him. It wasn't manmade. It was beyond natural. And though it wasn't caused by this self-proclaimed priest, he knew it was through the priest's actions that he felt it.

This priest who served no god.

This priest who barely served himself.

This priest who sought dominion over blood and stone.

The demon, however, was neither of these things.

Arella finished.

She'd compiled the ingredients, mixed them as prescribed, said the words as best she could, and now leaned back and said to Chloe, "I think it's done. It's over."

"Is it?"

Arella had no supernatural tendencies. No psychic abilities. She could no more reach into the mind of another than teleport herself from this abandoned underground speakeasy back to her place in Brooklyn. She felt no change on the air, or in the ether, or in the aura of the earth. These were things she understood. Things she'd read about and talked about. She'd seen others perform mystifying feats involving their mind or magic or some science she couldn't comprehend. She had heard the stories of conmen and misfits. She believed some and not others.

She had believed Neve Spirito when she spoke about the gargoyle and the demons and the cathedral that had disappeared. And tonight, she had seen other things. She had her own story to tell.

But was it truly over?

She didn't know. She had no sense of any change. The gargoyles might still answer to that madman. And the madman must somehow still answer for what he'd done.

Chloe reached out. Something in her eyes, her expression, looked different. She put a hand on Arella's shoulder and gave her more warmth, more comfort, more understanding than she would ever have believed Chloe's hand was capable of giving.

"It might be," Chloe told her, answering her own question. "It might not. And I don't think there's anything else we can do from here."

Arella shook her head. "Probably not."

"We have go back," Chloe said. "To St. Lazarus'. To my son."

CHAPTER 32

Pierce backed away from the advancing demon.

It was bigger than he'd seen it before. More beautiful than the demon he'd seen before. Stronger. It demanded more of the environment around it, and it single-mindedly focused all its attention on one person.

Him.

Pierce still commanded his army of gargoyles. They flung themselves at the demon, but at this point they barely served as a distraction. The demon destroyed each in turn. The winged lion. The eagles. The dancer. The iron dragon, the stone dog, the twin marble phoenixes. All reduced to rubble.

Pierce moved backwards. He was afraid to turn and run. The demon might spring on him then, might reach out with an as yet unseen tentacle and snatch him by the ankle. It had already destroyed his wrist. He didn't think there'd be any healing from that. Only terror and the certainty of death kept the pain at bay. He had neither the time nor energy to conjure any spells of healing or even numbing.

He brought forth spikes from the ground, but the demon simply smashed them.

He called upon a plague of something—anything— but the demon didn't even notice the locusts.

He tried to rip open the fabric of reality and send the demon hurtling through space and time. Let him follow the cathedral to wherever it had ended up. Let him disappear with it and become, again, mere legend.

He might have reanimated Constantine if he believed he was capable. With the book, the book his friends had stolen from him, he might have been able to do so—but he would have needed time.

Time which he did not have.

Suddenly, all around them, the gargoyles ceased their attempts to obstruct the demon. They looked confused—if they looked anything at all. Some simply spilled over. Some dropped. A few ran, vanishing into the dark and the rain. At least one let loose with a blood-curdling cry Pierce didn't dare try to interpret.

Some of them turned on him.

Those, perhaps, remained in the demon's path. The thing continued to crush them. It was an unstoppable force. It looked utterly otherworldly, worse than the demons depicted in the books, worse than the ones he'd seen fighting on this site twenty years before.

And he had done this.

He had forced its transformation.

He had pushed it beyond the constraints of all humanity. Whatever remained, there was nothing of the man inside anymore.

Pierce backed into a wall. No, not a wall. His lower back hit the edge of his own altar. The first gargoyles had constructed this for him. It had tasted human blood, not just his, and traces of his magic still flowed through it.

Pierce grinned. He knew what to do. He knew how to save himself.

He clamored over the altar, across the stone, scraping his palms and knees as he went. The rain needled him. Thunder shook his bones. Lightning danced in his periphery. The demon stopped at the edge of the altar, not more than five feet away from him now.

Pierce thought about every little dream he'd ever had, every bigger kid who had crushed them, every authority figure that had told him no, every priest who had threatened him with hell and damnation.

Before he could draw upon all of that, before he could enact his plan, something happened behind the demon.

One gargoyle remained.

The original gargoyle he'd placed in this pit when he first cast his spell. The one that had not come to life when he'd beckoned it to do so.

It descended.

It descended like a little god.

The demon heard it. The demon turned. Its wings created an eddy in the air pressure, sending the driving rain in a confusion of directions. The gargoyle landed amidst the rubble strewn all about.

Pierce took advantage of the moment. He scrambled across the altar, dropping to the ground on the other side, to his knees, so that he might hide behind and beneath it. It would offer little protection, but that's not what he wanted from it. He started doing his work.

His shattered wrist made it difficult. Not that he couldn't focus. Not that the pain was too much to bear, though it was getting closer to that every moment. His fingers responded poorly to his mental commands. They flexed only halfway when he intended for more. They twisted in part of a direction when he demanded more.

Intention was important.

He relied on that fact now.

He glanced in the direction of the little gargoyle. It kicked aside stones that had once been other gargoyles and reached the head of the statue who had been fried by lightning. The woman. Its—mother?

That gave Pierce pause.

The gargoyle touched its mother's face. So childlike. So tender. Then it raised its head and released a roar to rival any tiger, any elephant, and behemoth, any monster to ever walk the earth. That little body should've been incapable of noise like that. It screamed, it leapt into the air, and it flung itself at the demon's face.

The demon seemed for a moment unsure of what to do.

This was by far not the biggest or most intimidating of the gargoyles. But as the focus of Pierce's intentions from the very start, it was very probably the strongest and therefore the most enduring. It couldn't be simply shattered.

The demon took a breath, apparently bracing for impact.

Then released a roar of flames. A torrent of fire spewed from its mouth, engulfing the little gargoyle entirely. The concussive force of the explosion drove the gargoyle backwards. It tumbled through the air. Under that rush of fire, not just flames but liquid fire, burning like napalm, coating the stone and bringing the heat even more intensely.

The gargoyle fell to the ground.

It cried out. A wail this time. Something to give the banshees pause.

The demon ceased its onslaught. The burning, blackened gargoyle, reduced to crawling, ruined in every possible way, struggled to reach its fallen mother. It curled into her arm, pulled the limb over itself like a blanket, and in that way—died. In the arms of its mother.

There would be no more reprieves. Pierce closed his eyes. In the back of his mind, he prayed, though he would never have admitted to it. He funneled every ounce of what was left of him into the spell.

The demon leapt.

The demon crashed through the altar. But it didn't shatter. It didn't break.

Instead, the demon splashed into the altar.

The stone altar had become like a liquid. The more the demon splashed within it, the more thoroughly the substance coated its limbs. The liquid, like black amber, slowed the demon. Reached into its crevices. Infiltrated everything there was about the demon—and started to solidify again.

CHAPTER 33

Chloe reached the scene first.

She saw the fire. She saw the demon—her son, not Rick, but still terrifying, still ungodly, still a grotesquery of humanity—succumbing to whatever the priest had done to the altar. It swallowed her son. It meant to consume him.

The priest rose unsteadily to his feet. He kept one misshapen hand close to his chest. With the other, he directed the assault on Chloe's son.

She felt helpless. Useless. Incapable of saving her son, just as she'd been incapable of saving her Rick two decades ago.

Except Rick had been a monster.

The monster struggling in this trap right now, that wasn't her son. Not really. That was something else that had swallowed her son whole. That wasn't Stephen anymore. Maybe there was no more Stephen to find.

The demon looked at her as though she should be able to do something.

She simply watched. Bore witness.

———

Arella followed Chloe to the makeshift altar. They had moved swiftly through the dark labyrinths below Manhattan. Chloe had known every turn and every step.

For the moment, Arella ignored Stephen. She wanted to be sure of the gargoyles. She wanted to keep the book protected. For the moment, the priest didn't know she carried it. She had plans and intentions, but none of those would matter if she didn't eventually get away from the barren lot of St. Lazarus' Cathedral.

The gargoyles, all the hundreds of little and big statues, had scattered. They'd gone away, perhaps back to what they'd been, perhaps utterly destroyed. The last two, a mother and child, clung to each other in the aftermath of all that had happened here.

All that was still happening.

The substance was more than Stephen could deal with, even as a demon. It mired him down. It entangled him and absorbed into him and—Arella had to look away.

Had to not think of it.

She saw the priest instead.

At that moment, he saw her. He saw the book in her hands. The Book of Lost Fates which fueled this nightmare.

He grinned at her. He lost interest in Stephen altogether and came for her. He moved quickly, though he cradled one ruined hand. He said things. Things like, "I need that." And, "I will kill you." And, "I will keep you as my plaything when I've razed this city."

He tightened his good hand into a fist.

A vine of some sort tangled Arella's ankle. There would be no running. No fleeing. Chloe was caught between getting closer to her son and keeping her distance. Whatever Arella did to protect herself now, it was on her and her alone.

By now, the priest was between her and Stephen. Close enough to reach out for her. He went for the book. He had already decided she wasn't much of a threat.

Clutching the book with both hands, the thick

volume with its leather binding, Arella swung it like a weapon and smashed the priest's face. He dropped back, stunned and hurt. She'd drawn blood from the corner of his lip. Maybe a tooth or two had flown away. She couldn't be sure.

This time, he lunged for her.

Arella tossed the book.

It stopped him in his tracks. Before he could even turn to follow the book's trajectory, it hit the shard of stained glass that backed the altar with a wet smack.

The demon pushed away from the book, pulling itself out of the untenable substance and burying the book within it. For a moment, it disappeared entirely from view. The priest snatched at it with his wounded hand.

The substance caught him and yanked him in.

He didn't have Stephen's strength or stamina. It enveloped him entirely. For a moment, he seemed to have the book in his hands. He cried out in triumph. The quickly solidifying liquid altar poured down his throat. He choked. He struggled to break free.

Stephen rolled away on the ground in his fullest, most frightening demonic form.

Without the priest's words and gestures to keep the altar pliable, it melted into stone. It shaped around the priest's limbs. Drove through his eyes, down his throat, into his every orifice. It ripped apart the book, and the book refused to go silently.

The priest tried to claw his way out, but found the stone quite inescapable.

While some of the alter remained with Stephen, the majority of it hardened around the priest. He became one of the statues he had intended to control.

Stephen, meanwhile, still struggled with the part of the altar that had him. It also encased him, but the substance stretched thinly to keep him. It couldn't get all of him. It trapped one of Stephen's legs. It had crawled halfway up Stephen's waist.

And now, Stephen, in his demonic form, was trapped.

Chloe rushed to him first.

•———•

"No," Chloe said, through tears and through rain and through an utter, unblinking clarity. "No, no, no." She repeated the word like a chant, like an incantation, like it might mean something. It wouldn't. Couldn't. The stone was unyielding. She had seen a creature in stone before. A creature in stone had slain her Rick.

And now, the stone had claimed her son.

"No!" she cried, louder, startling even Stephen. His head was clear of the reaches of the stone. But it looked at her without recognition. Without pity. With maybe a trace of fear.

She was projecting. Chloe knew it. She wanted to read those feelings, or the lack of them, into her son's expression. But the truth was, his demonic face was beyond her ability to interpret. The ridges were inhuman. The scars recent and fresh and still bleeding. Though the blood was red, it was not, strictly speaking, blood.

Arella pushed to Chloe's son. She was crying. Crying. Real emotions. She was saying something to her son, something Chloe could understand when she tried to listen. "You're still in there, Stephen." She spoke softly enough, the storm threatened to swallow every word. "It's not the demon inside you that's going to break you free."

Then Arella kissed Chloe's son.

⚬————⚬

It was soft. Tender. Impossibly meaningful.

It was everything Arella had inside her. She didn't know Stephen, hadn't known him for more than a day, truly, and she wasn't so quick to believe she was in love, that was a big thing and she was old enough to know it was special — but absolutely she loved him, she believed in him, she hoped and dreamt for him. She would stay by his side through whatever was coming next, because he still had to deal with the fact that there was a demon under his skin. He had to learn more than just control.

And he had been an extraordinary lover, demon or no. She wasn't about to give that up.

She kissed his demonic lips. For a moment, Stephen seemed confused by it, unsure of how he was supposed to react. His mouth was enormous now, so that she really only kissed his lower lip. If he kissed her back, he might crack her skull.

Instead, he touched her. He reached up with one arm, through the stone that had barely begun to reach that far, and touched her back. Tugged her closer.

And transformed.

⚬————⚬

Transforming back to human was not without pain, but it was nothing compared to what he'd just experienced. Stephen quickly came back to himself.

When his lips were his lips, when he truly felt Arella's mouth, he kissed her back and it was wondrous.

The transition back to human shrunk him to a human size. Inside the stone, he ripped free of its grasp. It no longer moved and flowed like a liquid. With some effort, and some help from both Arella and his mother, he extricated himself from the stone that had tried to engulf him.

He spared hardly a glance for the priest.

He was bloody and sore. He thought bones might still be cracked, and he would have to shift from human to demon and back again a few times to fully repair everything. For the moment, he didn't mind the pain. Arella supported him on one side, his mother on the other, and together they left the site of St. Lazarus' Cathedral for the last time as the storm choked itself to a finish.

EPILOGUE

Unseen and unnoticed, a woman, naked as the day she'd been born—which might have been today had it not been hundreds of years prior—held her infant close to her chest and slipped away from St. Lazarus' Cathedral. She didn't know what had happened or why, and she had no idea what would happen in the future. Her understanding of the world was limited, and in many ways tainted by the village where she'd lived previously, but those memories had mostly faded and she had no desire to bring them back.

She moved with stealth and rapidity, guided in part by her infant's urges. Their connection was well beyond physical. She felt the child's hunger, but also its desire for safety, and at least for now it led her through the underground to a speakeasy where people didn't go.

She would have to eat. Eventually. And drink. She recognized that there were old liquors still on hand here, but none of them would help her. First, her baby needed to feed. Her baby. Her infant that had maybe once been a gargoyle and maybe once had died in a fire with her for no real or honest reasons in a faraway place and long, long ago, was hungry.

She might not have been the true angel she'd briefly thought, but she could act as the angel the baby needed.

In the safety and darkness of the speakeasy, the infant fed at her breast.

How much time had passed before Pierce became aware of his surroundings? Hours, at least. Days, maybe years, maybe even centuries. He had no sense of time, and there was nothing to see in the gloom. He was a statue now, a statue kept in a secured basement somewhere and incapable of movement. He tried to reach out with his mind, to project himself astrally, but nothing happened. He was stuck, thoroughly and completely. He was hungry and tired and in pain, incapable of sleep except when it came in stretches of uncertain hazy awareness, a kind of sleeplike state that never took away any of the agonies he felt. Pierces of stained glass windows were embedded into him, forever stabbing and slicing and scraping within a stone casing that surrounded him from within and without.

He tried to move.

He tried for a long, long time to move.

He tried to break free. He tried to animate himself. He tried to reach within and find The Book of Lost Fates he knew had been trapped within this same prison.

He tried to imagine himself anywhere else.

And he tried to die.

Nothing worked. Nothing moved. Nothing eased his pain.

After some time recovering, and exploring each other in ways Stephen had hardly imagined before, in ways that went a long way to satiating the beast within him, he and Arella boarded a flight to Florida to visit the only other person on earth they knew had faced demons and a gargoyle of her own.

Neve Spirito picked them up at the airport.